GRANT MY LAST REQUEST

Published in paperback in 2018 by Sixth Element Publishing
on behalf of Beryl Robinson

Sixth Element Publishing
Arthur Robinson House
13-14 The Green
Billingham TS23 1EU
Tel: 01642 360253
www.6epublishing.net

ISBN 978-1-912218-44-8

British Library Cataloguing in Publication Data. A catalogue record for this book is available from the British Library.

Printed in Great Britain.

GRANT MY LAST REQUEST

BERYL ROBINSON

Also by Beryl Robinson

A Life Of Consequence

CHAPTER ONE
AUSTRALIA

SOUNDS LIKE A DEATH KNELL

"Well, if my eyes don't deceive me, if it ain't Mrs Cloverley. As I live and breathe. You're like a h'apperition. We thought you was dead," the voice said.

Startled, Hannah turned too quickly, stumbling into the man's arms as he stretched out to steady her. She hadn't turned because she recognised his voice, she hadn't, but it was the mention of her old name. There was terror in her eyes that she knew would give her away so she looked to the ground until she could find her composure. Taking a deep breath Hannah tried not to falter as she spoke. "Oh you gave me a start, sir. I didn't hear you come up behind me. You have the wrong person. My name is Mrs Phelan."

"Aye well that might be yer name now but I never forget a face. The name's Samuel Fletcher. I was a stable lad when your da worked at Holdham Hall." He held out his hand. As an afterthought he continued, "Eh your da was a drinker, middled with some strange folk, as you know, but he knew 'bout 'orses."

Hannah didn't reciprocate. She felt the colour drain from her face at the mention of her father. Her throat was dry but she had to speak. "As I said, sir, you have the wrong person. My father never worked at, I'm sorry, I don't know the place you mentioned."

The man wouldn't be put off. "I remember you would come to the gate with your ma before you married Thomas Cloverley..." He was about to go on when one of the stall holders came over to Hannah's side.

"Everything alright, Hannah?"

"Yes, oh yes," she replied, feeling sick at the mention of her first husband's name. Composing herself as best she could, she continued, "This gentleman seems to have me mixed up with someone else."

Samuel Fletcher took his leave but his parting words, "I'm sure we'll meet again. We have a lot to talk about, after all," left Hannah cold.

She thought she had got away with it, escaped to the other side of the world to make a new life. Now she was a widow with two, three children. Would the nightmare start again? She didn't remember the man, Samuel Fletcher. He would have been just a boy then, but he obviously knew her father. What did he know? That was the question she needed an answer to. She couldn't think.

Hannah watched him go, her heart beating loudly in her ears. Her hands grabbed at the bodice of her dress as her legs gave way and she fell. She wanted to shut her eyes and will her life to end but she couldn't leave her beloved children as orphans. Hannah was brought back to the present when she heard the blacksmith taking irons from the fire. The striking of the hot metal sounded like a death knell.

As she lay in bed, the tightness in her chest was akin to a Gordian knot which threatened to choke her. She had woken in the darkness to her own sobbing, struggling to breathe. She was soaked in tiny rivulets of sweat that quickly cooled on the skin, making her shiver though the room was warm. Her nightmares had started again after the death of her second husband Mickey Phelan. They were back with a vengeance since his untimely death and Hannah was afraid. Even after all these years her nights were haunted by her first husband Thomas Cloverley. His face was vague but she could again imagine his fat coarse hands violating her body as he beat and raped her.

Hannah thought she had left those memories of her past behind when she made her new life for herself in Australia. Since the meeting of Samuel Fletcher, her nights were filled with that moment when, with shaking hands, she held the gun at arm's length, pointing the barrel at her drunk startled husband. Then bang! She shot him on the side of the temple, blood spurting as he took one step toward her before falling to the ground. It was so clear in her mind, as though it was only yesterday.

So as the shadows moved around the room and Hannah waited for a new dawn, she prayed. She prayed to God telling him she was indeed sorry for what she had done but He knew why she had done it. She wasn't making excuses, promising never to sin again. Hannah gave an assurance she would be devout in her prayers. Didn't His teaching say even the darkest, blackest of sins would be forgiven if you were repentant enough? It worried her that her husbands' souls would meet though surely her first husband would be stoking the fires of hell. Hannah prayed, prayed like never before, begging for forgiveness at being a sinner. If only God would give her a sign that she would indeed be forgiven. It was all she asked.

Finally, breathing in and out slowly and deeply several times, the knot in her chest began to unravel. It was as though God had cut the knot himself. There was a release, a kind of peace within her. Today would be a new start. She would brazen out any conversations with Samuel Fletcher if she could, though she hoped never to see him again.

As the week went on toward Saturday, her nerves were in pieces. It wasn't anticipation of returning to the market, she didn't know what the word was, fear, terror. It was the unknown and she knew that everyone in the household was now aware of her short temper. It was with a heavy heart and dark shadows under her eyes that a reluctant Hannah filled the bogey, which Mickey had made to transport the children, with all sorts of items to sell. Over the weeks she had managed to buy and sell items making a profit, the money helping the family in a small way.

Hannah walked into town with Mary, her friend and saviour from the terrible conditions on the convict ship that had brought them to Australia. Mary had become a younger sister who had helped when the children, Amy-Rose and Kitty, were born but she now worked at the only hotel in town. Nearly everyone in the town of Cheapside had come through the correction facility but no one ever talked openly about their misdemeanours and although Hannah had shot and murdered her first husband, she thought she had got away with it, until now. Ridiculously she had been sent to Australia for a crime she hadn't committed, that of stealing a gold ring from a pawnbrokers when in fact it was her own wedding ring, but the judge had not believed her turn of events, sending her to Australia, leaving her son Daniel behind.

As Mary left for her work at the hotel, Hannah began unloading the items onto the old sheet in an effort to keep the dry earth off the clothes. Now she was alone, the trauma of meeting Samuel Fletcher left her as strained as the sleepless nights, as well as being unusually quiet. She didn't know how long she would be able to keep the conversation with him to herself. The knowledge of what he may or may not know left her fit to burst. She strained her ears for his voice, though it was his words that resonated with her. The other stallholders shouted good humoured words to anyone close which made her smile though her eyes continually searched along the main street.

Hannah was relieved when another Saturday was over and she hadn't come upon Samuel Fletcher again, her mood lighter as she walked home with Mary. She still felt she would have to talk to someone about her predicament before she lost her mind.

They were almost home before Mary asked if she was alright and she replied that she had felt a little faint but would be fine once they were home.

As the weeks raced by, Hannah still couldn't settle, every Saturday becoming an ordeal. She had become short with the children especially Amy-Rose who was becoming a proper madam. She made the decision that she would have to try to explain her predicament to her friends so they understood why she was so upset and out of kilter with herself. There was a small feeling of relief at making that decision and the hope that they would understand. The house and land had been purchased when Hannah married Mickey Phelan along with their friends Lizzie and Adam Quinn. It was the only way they could afford to buy a house and, although it was a bit of a squeeze with their growing families, it had worked well until now. She wondered how it would work when she divulged her previous life and the revelation that she had killed her first husband.

After they had finished their meagre meal, Hannah cleared her throat. "I'm so sorry for my behaviour over the last few weeks and I owe it to you all to try and explain."

"Before you do," Lizzie said, grabbing Adam's hand, "can we tell you our news?"

Hannah nodded simply because she didn't know where to start.

"We are going to have a brother or sister for Joshua." Lizzie grinned at Hannah and Mary.

Hannah tried to look happy for the family while Mary made enough noise for both of them. It was what they said following their news which perturbed Hannah.

Adam spoke quietly. "I, we appreciate your loss, Hannah, really we do but we will not manage on the money coming in once Lizzie gives up work."

Hannah screamed, making the children cry. "My loss, you appreciate my loss? My husband isn't lost, he's dead and buried. My girls have no father." She spat the words out. "You make it sound as though I have mislaid Mickey but he's never coming back. Do you hear me, he's never coming back. My son is as good as dead to me, abandoned in England, no husband, no money. My life could hardly get any worse and now this." Her voice broke into a sob as she thought of Samuel Fletcher.

There was silence for several minutes before Lizzie reached out for Hannah's hand. "We know how hard this must be for you, Hannah, but just listen. Adam thinks we might be able to sell the land at the side of the house. If we could just separate it into a big enough plot for someone to build on, people are moving further out of town all the time. All we ask is that you think about it. Will you do that?"

Hannah nodded but once the children were settled for the night she excused herself and went to bed. She hadn't told them about Samuel Fletcher and that was probably for the best. As she lay listening to the girls sleeping, tears rolled down her face. When she had married Mickey she thought that she would be happy, and she had been very happy. She always felt that if her beloved son Daniel had been with her then she could have made a good life for them in Australia. Now her life was spiralling out of her control. Praying quietly, she asked God to grant her last request promising never to ask for anything again, to bring Daniel to her and make sure Samuel Fletcher stayed out of her life. She knew that this was asking for two things but they both went together. She knew she was asking for a lot but she would try and be a good Christian. Sighing deeply, Hannah tried to get some much needed sleep. Whatever happened she would have to get on with her life for the sake of Amy-Rose and Kitty. They deserved better. How she wished her mother was close to her. She needed to feel loved and cared for, to take all the heartache away.

"What was it you wanted to say, Hannah? We sort of stole the show last night," Lizzie said over breakfast.

"Oh never mind, it was nothing," Hannah said, relieved that she had not spoken about her dilemma. She couldn't deal with the looks on their faces, nor the retribution it could bring, instead she tried to get on with her life as best she could but was more quiet than usual.

Instead she allowed Mary to entertain them in the evenings with the goings on in the hotel which was really a public house during the day and a brothel in the evening. Hannah wasn't happy about the girl working there but the money was a godsend, giving her breathing space. She had tried to get Mary to take money for herself but she had refused. If Mary noticed an atmosphere in Hannah she never commented.

Hannah hadn't seen anything of Samuel Fletcher and was beginning to think he was a figment of her tormented imagination.

Perhaps the relentless heat caused him to be a mirage brought about by guilt.

Weeks went into a month as Hannah felt the tension in her shoulders begin to slacken. She was back to something like her old self, talking to the other stallholders, smiling at their silly banter backward and forward. As she was waiting for Mary to arrive, she spotted Dennis O'Reilly who she hadn't seen since Mickey's funeral. He was one of a number of Irish who had travelled on the ship with her and Mary, all remaining friends though he had been closer to Mickey, being from the same country.

He was sheepish at first. "I must apologise for not being in touch. How are you managing, Hannah? Are the children well?"

They continued to chat generally in between Hannah serving customers.

"Adam is thinking about selling some of the land but it is difficult when the outback is claiming it quicker than we can clear it." Smiling, she explained that Adam was doing his best but he really wasn't good at practical things. Whatever he managed to do one weekend needed doing again the following one.

It was as Dennis was about to take his leave that the nightmare by the name of Samuel Fletcher arrived, speaking loudly. "Mrs Phelan, Mrs Phelan, good to see you again."

Hannah glared at him in horror. How dare he stride up to her as though he was a friend? Not to be put off, he put his hand out to Dennis.

"Samuel Fletcher, I'm an acquaintance of Mrs Phelan from England. I worked with her father."

Hannah's mouth was agape and she was about to protest but Dennis took his hand. "Dennis O'Reilly." He turned to Hannah. "I really must be off but hopefully I will see you soon."

Taking his leave, Hannah was left looking at the man she disliked immensely.

"Mr Fletcher, you really must stop talking as though we were friends. I don't know you and neither did my father. Now if you don't mind..." She didn't finish.

"Come now, my dear, you can keep up this pretence or we

can indeed become friends which could be mutually beneficial to us both. I hear you have recently been widowed so life must be difficult for you?"

"I really don't wish to continue this conversation. I bid you good day!" Hannah turned from him picking up some clothes that she shook out before putting them back on the ground. She watched him walk away but was dismayed to see him stop to talk to Dennis on the main street. He was holding the horse's halter while patting its neck. She looked up when she heard him laughing loudly and he had the cheek to wave to her as he went on his way.

Her life was becoming more and more complicated and she didn't know what to do about it. When she came up with one solution, she was faced with another. Now that man was talking to people she thought of as friends. He could be telling Dennis anything. She would have to continue to keep up the pretence that she had never seen him before, and she hadn't, so that wasn't a lie. It was his word against hers. Surely people she cared about would believe her.

Fortunately Mary arrived and the two of them packed up and did a little shopping before heading off home.

CHAPTER TWO
ENGLAND
THE LETTER

Adele was woken to a loud banging on the cottage door. Putting her hand to the other side of the bed she realised her husband Daniel wasn't there. The early morning light was streaming through the curtains as she jumped out of bed.

"Hang on, hang on," she called, climbing down the ladder before putting her coat over her nightdress.

The voice of Mr Carter the coal merchant boomed, "Has he slept in? The horse is banging on the stable door and the cart's not set up."

Adele was still half asleep as she opened the door. "He's not here," she said. "I thought he had already gone out on his round. I must have slept in. I must get the boy up for school or he will be late."

Mr Carter followed her into the cottage as Adele called up the steps for young Daniel. The silence was embarrassing for both of them so she climbed up the ladder and into the boy's room. The bed had been slept in, she knew that. Hadn't she put him to bed herself last night, but where was he now? Returning to the small room, she just knew something wasn't right but she didn't want to voice it to Mr Carter.

As she turned to speak to him, the light caught something sitting on the table. Daniel's wedding ring. And what was that with it? She moved forward, realising there were two letters, one addressed to her and one to Mr Carter which she passed to him.

"Oh my Lord, my Lord," Adele wept, clutching her throat as though she was being choked as she fell into a chair. "No, no, he can't do this to me, oh no."

Mr Carter was no good with this kind of thing, weeping women, so shouted for his son to go and get the Mrs. He read his letter again, not wanting to make eye contact with Adele. As soon as his wife appeared, wiping her hands on her apron, he made his excuses to sort out the rounds. His older son would have to miss school to go out on Daniel's round, he said to no one in particular.

Passing the letter to his wife, he left the two women to it, shaking his head as he left. After reading it, Mrs Carter placed her hand on Adele's shoulder but moved it as though she had been struck as the woman began screaming like a fishwife.

"It's that whore. He's taken the boy to that whore. I knew he was up to something when we got that letter saying her husband was dead. I'll get the polis on to him. He can't take that boy away from me. He's my life." Snarling, Adele continued with her tirade. "He is my ward. He was left in my care, not his. He can't do this to me."

Mrs Carter was at a loss as to what to say so began raking the fire ready to re-light it to make a cup of tea. That was all she could think of as Adele was still shouting all kind of profanities while banging her hands on the table. As she moved toward her to comfort her, Adele swept her hand across the table, not only knocking the wedding ring onto the floor but the plates, a candle and the ink pot which splattered across the stone floor and up the wall.

"Come now, come now. Let it out, that's it." Mrs Carter attempted to put her arms around Adele's shoulder but was pushed away.

"Get out. Go on, get out. I just want to be left alone. Go on leave me," Adele screamed at the woman.

Worried about leaving Adele alone in this state, Mrs Carter asked, "Can I get someone for you? I could get one of my lads to take a message on their way to school if I catch them?"

"Just go," Adele snapped.

"I'll come back later and see if you're alright," Mrs Carter said, heading toward the door.

"Alright, alright. I'll never be alright. He has taken everything from me. He couldn't give me a child and now he has taken the boy from me. He was my child and I loved him." Adele began screaming again.

Alone, Adele cried loudly for a long time. Not for Daniel, her husband, she knew he had never been really happy. She had forced his hand to marry her and now she had got her just desserts some would say. The only light in her life had been that young boy. She had cared for him, nurtured him and yes, loved him. The latter surprised her as he was Hannah's child but that didn't matter. It seemed God provided her with the one thing Daniel couldn't and now he was gone.

"I'll get myself away to see Pastor John. He will know what to do," she said loudly. "I must have that boy back. Daniel can go to hell."

Washing her hands and face in cold water, she put on her good dress. If she went now, she might catch him before he went out to see his parishioners. She wanted to speak to him in private, though she knew her business would soon be all round the town. Fifteen minutes later Adele had her coat and bonnet on as she hurried out of the yard toward the town.

Adele almost marched though the streets neither looking left or right. She pushed past people in her hurry to speak to John. The letter was in her coat pocket and as Mrs Parr, the housekeeper, opened the door, Adele pushed her way into the hall. She yelled unceremoniously at the housekeeper asking if the Pastor was at home.

The noise brought John from his study. He was almost pushed aside as Adele rushed into the room. As he put his hands out to slow her down, she fell into them almost knocking them both to the ground. He motioned to the housekeeper to bring a tray of tea before leading Adele to a seat. Her tears unnerved him. He had always thought of her as a stoic woman who wasn't given to hysterics. She didn't speak but continued to cry as she handed the now crumpled letter from her pocket.

"I'm sorry, my dear. What will you do? Will you be able to manage financially?" John regretted saying the latter immediately the words left his lips.

"I don't care about that. I just want the boy back. I don't care if I never see Daniel again. That boy was my life." Adele continued to sob.

John sat for a while longer, pouring out two cups of tea, handing one to Adele before he continued. "We need to look at the legalities of this, Adele. The boy isn't yours and according to this letter he is to be taken back to his mother. I don't think you would have any rights, I'm sorry."

"The polis can look for them. After all, he is my ward, you know that. His mother gave him to me to care for. His mother is a criminal. You went to London to look for her years ago, you know where the ships would be docked, we could go and look for them." She was rambling on somewhat incoherently.

"Slow down, Adele. You had no legal right to the boy, did you? It was your husband who knew his mother and I am sure the polis would agree that the best place for the boy is with his mother and siblings. I'm sorry, look, let's pray for a safe journey for them and I will write to Hannah to ask her to let us know when they arrive so we know the boy is safe."

The sound of Hannah's name sent Adele into a frenzy of screaming which John didn't know how to deal with so he just let her get on with it. Eventually she calmed down, blowing her nose on her handkerchief before gasping, "I don't want you to contact her." She almost spat the words. "She's up to no good, mark my words. Well, let her get a shock when she finds the pair of them on her doorstep. You're telling me I can't do anything about it? Daniel has taken everything away from me, everything I loved. I am left with nothing." Adele began sobbing again.

John thought it better not to say any more because she was right. That man had indeed taken everything from her. She should have never married him. It was Daniel's fault that Hannah had ended up in Australia in the first place. Men like him always seemed to have women falling for their charms but he couldn't see any good in him. He had never liked the man.

Adele stood, fastening her coat. "I thought you would be able to help me but I see that you can't."

"Look, I'm off to the workhouse," he said. "Come with me. I don't like the idea of you being on your own." He handed her the letter which she snatched out of his hand.

"No, no, I need to go home and look at the books before speaking to Mr Carter about running my share of the business, I'm sure I can manage that." She half laughed.

Deciding not to say more, John saw Adele out of the house and watched as she walked down the path, shoulders bowed. She seemed to have aged in those few moments. Perhaps throwing herself into the business would take her mind off things but it was a sad day for her to lose a husband and child in this way. She had been left in the lurch but at least she would have some kind of income from the business. He would pray for Adele, call in to see her tomorrow, give her a bit of time to get used to the idea of being alone.

Adele set about scrubbing the ink from the wall and floor, sobbing with each movement of her hands as the scrubbing brush moved backward and forward cleaning the slates. The floor finished, she began with the same vigour at the kitchen table. Pushing her hair back with wet hands before drying them on the rag, she looked for her next task. Going up to the bedroom, she collected the remains of Daniel and the boy's clothes, throwing them into a pile on the floor below. She would wash them before taking them to the workhouse sure someone would welcome them.

Her next job was to pick up all the bits and pieces in the garden which wanted burning but Daniel had never got round to. Well, she would, she thought as she watched the smoke rising to the sky. She jumped as Mr Carter called her name.

"Adele, come on, lass, enough. The Mrs has put some food on the table for you as I'm sure you haven't eaten today."

She didn't want to think about eating but allowed herself to be led into their overcrowded kitchen. The children sat staring at her, this woman who they hardly knew, but none of them spoke. Forcing herself to eat what had been put in front of her, she finished as quickly as she could so she could get away.

Adele was about to take her leave when Mr Carter finally spoke. "I'm sorry but I need to talk to you about the business as soon as you feel up to it. My boys can help in the short term, but the fact is it can only be for a few weeks. I can of course buy your share of the business, though I wouldn't be able to give you the full value. It's such short notice and with things already being tight. Have you given any thought as to what you might do with it?"

Adele listened, nodding her head. "Do with it? I intend to run the business, Mr Carter. I will find someone to do the delivery work, don't you worry about that. Just give me a few days to look over the books," she said determinedly. This was her only means of income now and she would have to see a solicitor to make sure her name was placed on the business.

She would never be beholden to a man ever again. She would make it work, after all she wasn't stupid, how difficult could it be to keep the books up to date? If Daniel had managed then she was surely more than capable. Lying in the marital bed, she watched the light turn to dark before she finally fell into an exhausted sleep.

For the next few days Adele worked like a dervish, washing, cleaning, just trying to keep her mind and body busy so she didn't have time to think. Pastor John had called briefly to see how she was getting on though their conversation was rather stilted. Adele explained what she was going to do to keep the business afloat.

"I may be able to help you with getting someone to work for you. I am going to the workhouse later. There is someone I think may be suitable. Can I send him to you?" he asked.

She agreed, more to get him out of the cottage as she wanted to be left alone. "Yes, I suppose that would be fine but it would be difficult if they remained at the workhouse and I can't have someone living here."

The bedding was billowing on the line in the soft breeze as she picked up the business accounts. She had hardly started looking at them when there was a single rap on the door making her jump. She didn't get visitors and hoped it wasn't Mrs Carter attempting to befriend her, she could do without the pity. Stood in front of her was a man so painfully thin, his clothes threadbare, that she could almost see right through him.

"I erd yer ad a job going, Mrs. The Pastor sent me and I came straight away like," he said, removing his cap and holding out his hand but taking it back quickly.

Adele looked at the poor man. He would never be able to do the heavy manual work of filling and lifting the coal and wood sacks on and off the cart. "Oh I'm sorry, it's really heavy work." She looked at the poor man who looked almost ready to collapse at any minute. She didn't know why but she felt incredibly sorry for him and against her better judgement invited him in for a cup of tea for his trouble. She placed several spoons of sugar in the mug before slicing a piece of rabbit pie that she put on a plate and passed to him. Neither spoke but the man watched her as she sat at the end of the table where the books had been placed.

"Thank yer, Mrs, it's very kind of yer," he said as he picked at his food.

It surprised Adele. She thought he would wolf it down as he looked so hungry but he ate somewhat delicately.

"I know aye look as though a wind would blow me over but I'm stronger than I look," he said hopefully.

"Working as a coal man is very physical work," Adele replied. "At the moment I don't even know if I can afford to employ anyone."

"If yer give us a chance, Mrs, I won't let yer down," the man said before draining his mug. "I'd work for bed and board on a trial like."

"Oh no, there's nowhere for anyone to stay." Adele was shocked as she hadn't thought too much about that. She watched as the poor man stood to take his leave. That's all she could say about him, the poor man.

"Ta for yer time and the grub. Mrs." He went to shake her hand but thought better of it again, picking up his cap instead.

After closing the door, she poured herself another cup of tea and picked up the accounts again. They were basic. Daniel always said he wasn't much of a scholar but he had managed to keep them quite neat and tidy. Looking at the top of the list, she saw the rent on the cottage and stabling for the horse, as well as the weekly payment for the coal and logs. She wondered how much mark up Mr Carter made on this. Perhaps she could ask him. She could always plead ignorance or try to use her womanly guile. There was also the cost of feeding the horse. Daniel had bought the horse and cart with the money he made for the sale of his town house years ago. He gave her a generous allowance for food and anything she may need for herself or the boy. She thought it was generous until she saw what money came into the business. His mark up for what he charged for coal and logs, although not huge, was significant. He did sell large quantities around the area. If the figures were accurate, where was the rest of the money?

Going into the garden to bring in the washing, she heard someone chopping wood in the stable. The cart wouldn't be back yet so she went to have a look. It was the man who had called an hour earlier. She watched him, his shirtsleeves rolled up while lifting the axe above his head before splitting the wood into kindling.

He stopped when he saw her. "Just wanted to repay yer kindness, Mrs. I've filled what spare bags I could find. The rest I'll just leave in a pile."

"That's very kind of you but I don't want to keep you Mr…? I'm sorry I didn't get your name?" Adele asked, impressed with the amount of work he had completed in such a short period of time.

"Edward, Eddie Dawson," he replied, wiping his hands on his trousers intending to offer his hand for a third time but thinking better of it.

"I don't want to keep you, Mr Dawson."

"I'll be off then but if yer find any work, Mrs, I'd be grateful. I'll be at the workhouse until I find summat." He walked off, hoping she would call him back but she didn't.

Adele looked around the empty stable. Where would Daniel hide money? She smiled at her own joke, as she was looking after the horse had bolted so to speak. Surely he would have taken everything with him, after all his note had made it perfectly clear that he wouldn't be back. She tried one or two of the bricks on the back wall but couldn't loosen them. While she was looking, she couldn't get that man out of her mind, not Daniel, no he was gone for good, but Eddie Dawson. He was so keen to help even though he looked as though he would drop down dead at any moment.

She had told him that there was nowhere for him to live but she had an idea. Going to the side of the stables, she looked up the moss covered stone steps she knew led to a room used for storage though she had never been inside. Placing her feet carefully on the steps, she climbed, holding onto the wall. Trying the door, it was stiff but unlocked and it eventually opened. The room wasn't as long as the stables below though there was a small window at one end looking out onto the yard. If it was cleaned out, she could put some furniture in but it would only take a bed and a small table and chairs at a push.

With the seed of accommodation in her mind, Adele returned to the cottage, picking up the accounts again as she worked out how much she would have each week once all the bills had been paid. Counting what money Daniel had left her, she wondered if she would be able to afford any second hand furniture. There was only one way to find out but first she would need to put it to Mr Carter, though she was determined to have her way.

Adele heard Mr Carter's return by the clip clopping of the horse into the yard. She was in a rush to speak to him but thought it prudent to wait until he had finished his evening meal when he may be more relaxed and she didn't want an invitation to join them again. She tried picking at her cold meal but couldn't settle so paced the few steps back and forward.

She could wait no longer so grabbed the account book, crossing the yard before banging on the door quite loudly. She was invited to sit at the table as Mrs Carter pushed her sons out of the way, almost falling off the end of the bench.

"I've looked through the accounts, Mr Carter, but as things stand

I won't be able to employ anyone if they live out. I couldn't pay the wages they would require," Adele stated. Mr Carter was about to speak but she stopped him. "I have come up with a solution if you bear with me. The room above the stable isn't used. I could clean it out. I could provide some of the meals."

"Oh I don't think that would be suitable. It's very small. I wouldn't be happy having strangers about the place." He swept his hand across the table.

"Well, Daniel and I were strangers once, Mr Carter, and we seemed to muddle along fine. As I said, I wouldn't be able to employ a worker if they lived out, it would just cost far too much. I could ask my friend Pastor John to look over any suitable candidates and of course you would have some say in my choice. I can't think of any other solution to my dilemma." Adele continued as she managed to squeeze a tear from her eye which she allowed to roll down her cheek.

"All right, my dear," Mr Carter said uncomfortably. He didn't want any more hysterics. "As long as I can speak to them before the job is offered. Do you have anyone in mind?"

"As a matter of fact, I do, but I will need to check his credentials with the Pastor, as I said. I would take him on trial, of course, with your agreement." Adele was confident she had won the first battle. Standing, she said, "I will need to provide some furniture. Could you collect it on the cart?"

"Of course, my dear, just let me know when." Mr Carter opened the door for Adele to leave, feeling he had been backed into a corner.

CHAPTER THREE
ANOTHER CHAPTER

The following morning, Adele was up and out early, hoping to catch Pastor John at home. If the conversation went as planned she would walk with him to the workhouse to speak to Mr Dawson. The housekeeper took a step back when she opened the door to Adele, not wanting to be pushed out of the way.

"Good morning," Adele said pleasantly. "Could I have a word with the Pastor?" As she saw John in the hallway she continued, "Can I apologise to you both for my outburst. It was the shock. I am truly sorry."

John took her arm to usher her into his study, talking for several minutes as Adele explained her plans. They left the house together, continuing to talk as they walked past the church, through the graveyard before reaching the workhouse gates that still had the family crest on the ironwork. She had always gone through the side gate and directly into the hospital ward when she came to read to the patients. The gravel driveway was wide enough for traps to pass but the front door was initially hidden by a now defunct water fountain. Someone had thought to fill the pond with plants at some time but now it was full of rubble and weeds. Things that were no longer needed, Adele thought, a bit like the poor inmates.

It was a foreboding building that had originally been a manor house but as the town grew around it the owners had moved on. The stable and coach house had been converted into rooms for the men while the main house was for women, children, a hospital and office.

John spoke briefly to the woman behind the desk who provided them with the file on Eddie Dawson. There was little information other than he had returned to the town where he had been born when his parents were in service. It seemed that he had lost his job when his wife became ill, dying a few months ago.

There was a smell of boiled cabbage combined with mould and antiseptic, making Adele wrinkle her nose, while the constant echo of footsteps made her want to put her hands to her ears. The odour of sickness in the hospital was bad enough, though the windows were always open however inclement the weather. The office felt oppressive with the smell of body odour as the woman moved, trying to tidy the desk, and Adele realised the smell was coming from her.

"There might be a problem with Mr Dawson, Adele," John stated tapping his finger on the paper. "The man came to the workhouse with his son who is aged fourteen. They are working in the garden." Without waiting for a reply, he turned to the woman and said, "We'll go out and speak to him. I'll be back shortly." He shepherded Adele out into the corridor, saying, "Let's sneak out here rather than going all the way round. I won't tell if you don't." He laughed.

Adele wasn't really listening. She couldn't take a man with a boy, there wasn't enough room. There were a large group of men working in what seemed to be a vegetable plot. Some were digging while others raked over newly made beds. Mr Dawson stopped when he saw the pair walking down the narrow path between the plots. They stopped to talk to the ganger who pointed in his direction so he removed his cap, put down his spade and walked toward them.

"Good morning, Mr Dawson." Adele wanted to speak before John. "I didn't realise you had a child with you and this makes things rather difficult. I have accommodation at the coal merchants but it really isn't big enough for two and I certainly couldn't manage to pay two wages."

John put his hand on Adele's arm. "Let's not be too hasty. Let Mr Dawson speak."

"I thank thee for thinking of me, Mrs. I never mentioned the lad cause I never thought you would offer me the job. He could 'elp with the cart and he's good wiv 'orses. He's old enough to leave school. We would work for the one wage, Mrs, as long as we could be together. He's a good lad and we'll not let yer down if yer just give us a chance."

Adele had warmed to this man for some reason. Yes, he was rough round the edges but seemed a good worker and keen. "Come up tonight with your son, Mr Dawson, and have a look at the accommodation and perhaps we could come up with something though Mr Carter would have to agree. It would be on a trial basis, mind," she added.

"Thanks for the chance, Mrs. We won't let yer down. I'm sure the room will be better than here, no offence, Pastor." Mr Dawson smiled. "We'll be there around seven."

As they walked back along the path, John said, "Are you sure about this, Adele? It might be upsetting for you to see a boy around the place? Do you want me to be there when you see them?"

"No thanks, I can manage on my own. Mr Carter will have to give the once over anyway though I am sure he won't cause any problem if I am happy. His house is full of boys so I will have to get used to it."

Adele got home and immediately changed into her old clothes before putting the fire on and the kettle on the hook to warm some water. While she was waiting for that, she took the brush to sweep out the room above the stables. Dust and cobwebs were everywhere. She wasn't sure if mice had ever made a home there but she had no time to worry about that. The old items were carried down into the stable. She would leave them for Mr Carter to sort out. In no time at all she washed the small window which immediately let in more light. Using the dirty water, she mopped the floor but it was still smeared with dirt. Rinsing the bucket under the tap in the yard, she filled it again with cold water carrying it back up the steps. The second time it looked a little better. Looking at her hard work, the room looked slightly bigger now it was empty. She thought she would be able to squeeze two single beds at one end though they wouldn't have much room between them. One of them could have young Daniel's as she wouldn't be requiring it again. She mentally made a note that she would need another bed, bedding, two chairs, a table as well as smaller items like a lamp, crockery and cutlery, she didn't want them using hers. Closing the door behind her, she returned to her own cottage for a welcome cup of tea, her throat dry from the dust.

Mr Dawson and his son Frank, who was a younger version of his father, arrived on time and were delighted with the tiny room. Mr Carter wasn't sure what to make of the pair though he could see that Adele had already made up her mind. He knew from past experience never to argue with a woman who had made up her mind. He agreed that his son would accompany them on the round for the first week but then they would be on their own. They would be responsible for loading the cart each day but he would go through the rounds with them when they arrived later in the week.

Adele took the two of them back to the cottage, giving them a cup of tea and a slice of bread and dripping. They both ate hungrily though she knew they would have eaten before they left the workhouse. Once the wages were agreed and the meal arrangements sorted, Adele shook hands with both of them.

Within weeks of the two of them arriving, Adele had settled into a comfortable routine, providing them with breakfast on the six days they were working which included a flask of tea and bread for the day. Although she cooked an evening meal for them, they ate in their room; she wasn't ready to make small talk with anyone yet. On Sunday she made a roast dinner, allowing them to collect it after they had been to church. She didn't ask what their religious preferences were, assuming they were happy with the routine. Saturday was a short day and she often watched Mr Dawson doing their washing at the cold tap while his son cared for the horse, washing and cleaning its hooves before clearing out the stable.

They seemed happy enough and strangely so was Adele in her own way. She had never had money of her own, always beholden to Daniel and before that to her mother and she found the business going better than expected. Adele spent some money on buying herself a high backed chair that sat next to the fire where she could relax after her busy days. The old chairs had been squeezed into the stable room. Occasionally she would wander to the market in the square looking around the stalls and shop windows, purchasing little treats or frivolities. She had no friends to call on other than John, nor any relatives, finding herself looking forward to the brief conversation with Mr Dawson or Frank.

For the first time in her life she had responsibility for her own life and was not beholden to anyone. She didn't count Mr Carter because he was an equal partner in the business whether he thought so or not. She would make it work if only to prove to herself that she could.

CHAPTER FOUR
AUSTRALIA
HOW LIFE CHANGES

The following morning, it being Sunday, the women were getting the children ready for church when Hannah heard voices talking loudly to Adam who was already out on the land. She hardly dare go outside in case it was Samuel Fletcher or the polis. She didn't know which would be worse.

She laughed somewhat hysterically when she realised it was Dennis with Mickey's other friends who had arrived in Australia with them, John Boyle, Thomas McCarthy and William O'Connell. Also with them was the man, Samuel Fletcher, who was patting Dennis on the back as though they were good pals. There was much laughter as they struggled to lift two heavily pregnant goats off the back of the cart. William explained that the animals would eat most of the vegetation but they would have to be roped to a stake otherwise they would eat the crops. They would also provide milk.

The men were evasive as to how they had acquired the animals, telling the families not to ask too many questions. Amy-Rose and Joshua wanted to pet the goats, squealing with delight as they touched them, protesting loudly when they were led away to wash their hands before setting off for church.

Hannah couldn't speak. That man was getting into her life and there didn't seem to be a thing she could do about it. He talked to the others quite freely and the Irish were always keen to make new friends. He waved toward her, which she ignored, wishing he had never come across her at the market.

While saying her prayers in church, Hannah didn't ask for any more help. What was the point? He didn't listen or He had a wicked sense of humour, one she didn't like. All she wanted was to be left in peace to bring up her children but obstacles were always in the way. But no more, she would not suffer the torment anymore. If that man came near her, she would make it clear she wanted nothing to do with him, and continue to do so until he gave up.

By the time they returned home several hours later, the waste land looked completely different. A pen had been built at the side of the veranda to house the animals overnight. William seemed an expert, explaining they would need the pen cleaning daily and this could be used on their crops as fertiliser. Some of the dry grass they had forked into a pile that could be used for bedding. They would need to look out for snakes, especially when the kids were born, he stressed. William showed them how to fork the grass and milk the animals. They were now busy measuring the land to be sold. Fence posts had been laid out ready to be dug into the red soil.

Hannah couldn't bear to watch the man staring at her so she retreated into the house while she asked Mary to take out mugs of water. Trying to keep busy, Hannah heard Mary laughing loudly as Dennis said something. She saw out of the open window Mary pushing him playfully before taking the mug out of his hand. Surely she couldn't see Dennis as a prospective partner. He must be almost forty years old, a pleasant enough man but rather dumpy if she were being truthful. Regardless of all that, she was eternally grateful to the Irish men for all their help. Samuel Fletcher was another matter altogether. What were his intentions, Hannah thought.

It was late in the afternoon when the men finally left, Hannah came out holding Kitty tightly to her as she waved them off.

It was Mary who mentioned his name first. "You have an admirer, Hannah. Samuel Fletcher seems smitten with you. He didn't stop mentioning you all afternoon."

"Shut up, shut up. That man is trouble, let me tell you. Keep away from him. He is a liar. I'm not sure what he is up to but he is spreading falsehoods about me and my life in England. He professes to know me and my father but it's all lies," Hannah shouted. "Now let's hear no more about him."

"Alright, there's no need to shout at me. I was only saying," Mary replied, upset at Hannah's tone.

"I'm sorry, Mary. It's just upsetting seeing Mickey's friends and him not being here." She hated lying to the girl. It was made worse when Adam joined in.

Looking directly at her, he said, "It may not be a bad thing to think about marrying again. It would give you and the children some security as well as helping with money worries. The man seemed pleasant enough."

He was about to go on when Hannah screamed at him. "Marry again? You make it sound like a commodity. I'll never marry again, do you hear? I thought we were friends." She looked directly at Adam and for the first time realised that she didn't much like him. He made out that he was helping but he wasn't and she knew he had a cruel streak in him. "If you don't want to help, that's fine, just give me the money Mickey put into this house and I'll find somewhere else for us to stay, and it certainly won't be with that man."

As usual it was Lizzie who tried to calm them down. "Come on, all of you. We're all tired. Let's just clear up and say no more about it there is no need for anyone to move out, is there?" She looked at both Adam and Hannah but neither responded.

Hannah gave in first, walking away and up to her room where she sat on the bed. What was happening to her? Even her friends seemed to think she knew that man when she could no longer bear to speak his name. If only she could find out what he knew. She may be worrying unnecessarily but she would never know unless she called him out. It was getting her nowhere and she couldn't keep retreating to her bedroom every time she thought she was going to blurt out how he knew her.

Instead she returned to the kitchen and took both Amy-Rose and Kitty to look at the animals in the pen, where they took food from their hands and they squealed happily. This was what she had to focus on, her girls.

Hannah still said her prayers each night but they were general. She didn't think God was listening to her ramblings any more. Her life wasn't perfect. She tried her best but it wasn't long before her faith in him was tested again. They had managed to sell the plot of land to an agent. They knew they would probably get more if they sold it themselves but they needed money quickly. He told them that this area used to be called the empty quarter but as the town was becoming overcrowded, people were happy to move further out. Much further and they would be in the outback, where the dusty road became nothing more than a track before the trees and bushes reclaimed it. A price was agreed and it gave Hannah what she thought would be breathing space before looking for employment.

Adam and Lizzie saw how well the land had sold to the right of the house and they felt the smaller plot on the left could also be cleared to give them another income. As it was, it was too big to manage, and selling some of it would still leave them with a nice garden and vegetable plot as well as access to the stream for water. The big problem was Mickey's grave which was at the bottom and in order to get the best price for the land it would also need access to the stream. Adam left Lizzie to broach that subject as he couldn't face another slanging match with Hannah.

Lizzie suggested that they visit the church together and discuss the possibility of purchasing a plot in the graveyard and have a memorial service for Mickey. Hannah wasn't happy at the thought of moving her husband but knew that if she didn't, the others would blame her every time they were struggling financially. She felt that the best thing was to go along with it because at some time in the future she wanted to be away from the confines of this house and have somewhere just for her and the children, with Mary of course.

A few days later they were sitting in the parlour talking to the Reverend, a man Hannah didn't really care for. She certainly didn't see herself having any meaningful conversations as she had in the early days with Pastor John. This one's eyes were too close together, his eyebrows too bushy and he stared at her uncomfortably.

"When my husband died, I didn't have money to purchase a plot in the cemetery," Hannah said sadly as Lizzie held her hand. "Once our land is sold, I will be able to pay for a plot and service if that is possible?"

"Well your request is rather unusual, as it's not that long since your husband was laid to rest," the Reverend replied, "but I'm sure we can come to some arrangement."

Hannah knew what that meant; she would cover his palm with silver which would not be given to the church but go straight into his cassock pocket. Well, it didn't matter as long as she could do right by Mickey. He would understand even if no one else did. "It's over six months," Hannah replied sadly.

Walking back along the dirt road toward home, Lizzie linked Hannah's arm. "I'm so proud of you, Hannah. That wasn't an easy conversation to have and you have borne Mickey's passing with grace while being strong for your babies. I know you will never forget him but life will get easier if we all stick together."

Hannah couldn't respond, only squeeze her friend's arm.

Lizzie was due to leave the school shortly and although Hannah had asked to take over her job she had been refused. The law on working was the same as in England, she was told, so married women were prohibited from working. Cheapside now had enough immigrants arriving for men to take up the posts. She had tried to protest that she was a widow who needed to earn a living, they knew she was a good worker, but the school board would hear none of it.

Life in the household was busy with cooking and baking ready for the festive season as never before. They had all agreed to invite the Irish men and their families for a meal to thank them for their help and kindness in helping to sell the land. Thomas McCarthy and William O'Connell were both married with children, while John Boyle was courting a young girl named Nancy and asked if she could come along.

Dennis arrived alone but brought a flagon of ale to have with the meal. Hannah realised that this was now her extended family.

It was a busy few weeks leading up to Christmas 1873. All the land was fenced off and sold. Mickey's body had been interned in the churchyard. His Irish friends had arranged the digging and removing of his body, which Hannah didn't want to see so set off with Mary to walk to the church. Lizzie, who was now heavily pregnant and struggling in the heat, remained at home with the children. The men followed the cart solemnly to the churchyard and after a brief service Mickey was reburied in a new plot with the original wooden cross.

There was muted joy and laughter in the household on Christmas day as the children were given gifts. Hannah had made rag dolls for Amy-Rose and Kitty from scraps of material with buttons for eyes. Joshua was given a wooden top that she purchased with a job lot of items for the stall. She bought both Lizzie and Mary new stockings while Adam received a pair of socks. She was fortunate to receive a handkerchief with her initial embroidered from Mary and lace gloves from Lizzie. They all agreed it was the best Christmas ever, though the heat made it difficult to do anything. Something they all missed from England was the snow as it still seemed so silly to be hot in winter.

When Hannah received a letter from England, she felt that at last God had truly forgiven her sins and this was the best end to the year she could ever wish for. One day soon her son Daniel would finally be with her. The letter from Pastor John hadn't gone into too many details but it seemed her old friend Daniel Jerrold had left his wife, Adele, and was bringing her son to her. They had cared for her boy since she had been sent to Australia, though the letter didn't explain the reasons why they had decided to come to her now.

CHAPTER FIVE
ENGLAND

DANIEL JERROLD'S CONFLICT

Sitting on the train, Daniel wondered if he had made the right decision to take this child to the other side of the world. What did he know about it? Had Adele found the letter, which was little more than a note? Whatever, he knew it was too late. He could never go back.

He was a fool, leaving behind a good business, a home, a wife. The latter he realised not for the first time he didn't much care for. Perhaps he had never loved Adele, though once upon a time he thought he did. Once he cared about what he thought she could give him, a standing in the community. He was wrong. He would always be looked on as a traveller, an outsider who had never belonged in Kingsmead. He had never felt comfortable in his own home; it was always Adele's even though it was his money that had provided for them.

Even in the bedroom the bed was warm enough with two bodies but the imaginary bolster between them was icy cold. He had never taken her by force, even though it was his right. That wasn't his way.

He had only ever felt at home as a child living on the farm with his parents and siblings. Then later, in the forest with his good friend, a grandfather to him, Albarn Tamblyn.

The smoke from the engine was pouring past the carriage as they built up steam. He'd missed a sale here on the railway with the amount of coal he had seen shovelled into the engine before they set off. He could have made a fortune and bought a big house. Daniel gave a wry smile at the thought of being a gentleman in his own right. What was the point? He had no one to leave his fortune to.

Daniel retreated back into his thoughts. What had possessed him to think he could travel to the other side of the world with a child? He had never really bothered with Hannah's son, leaving his upbringing to Adele. He knew that he had been wrong, the boy should have been his responsibility from the start but as usual he took the path of least resistance. It was his fault Hannah had left the boy behind. She had paid a debt to release him from a prison sentence so he could have his life, but look at the cost. Her son had ended up in his household when Hannah was sent to Australia. It was over six years ago but he had never forgiven himself for her demise so when he received the letter informing them of her husband's death he knew he had to repay his debt. The only way he could do that was by taking her son to her but it had been an emotional reaction. His plan had not been best thought out. Perhaps he should have gone to London on his own to find a ship before returning to pick up the boy but would he have ever returned? Probably not. How would he have explained to Hannah why her son wasn't with him?

He put his hand to his head. What a mess he had made of his life. He should have gone to James and Primmy's at the public house in Dealham. They would have welcomed him and Hannah's boy while he thought things through. It was too late now.

Even Daniel was tired by the time they reached the dockside where he could see a number of ships and men bustling along the jetty. His empty stomach lurched as he remembered how he hated the river and travelling on the wherry. The ships were much bigger with a mountain of rigging to deal with. Stopping by the first man who was coiling rope, Daniel asked, "Do you know if any of these boats are heading to Australia?"

The man spoke without removing the pipe which he placed between his teeth. "No, mate, you need to be further down the dock, them boats are much bigger. These just hug the coast." He pointed further along the water's edge while Daniel nodded, putting one hand on the boy's shoulder.

The whole port was bustling with men wandering about plying their barrows as they moved goods along the dockside. He found a place for the boy to sit with the bundle, warning him not to move and not to speak to anyone.

Walking quickly, Daniel asked at the first ship, but no luck, it wasn't going to Australia. It was going to a place called America but he didn't know where that was so walked on. He asked at a few more ships until one seemed promising. The sailor told him to come back the following morning to speak to the captain but they were not due to sail for a few weeks.

He also asked the man if he knew anywhere close by which provided rooms, preferably a boarding house.

"There's a woman, Clara Heggerty, who has rooms but she usually asks for money upfront. It's in a sandstone house with a black door not far from the entrance to the docks. The rooms are quite clean and the grub excellent," the sailor said, pointing back toward the dock gates.

Daniel shook his hand and thanked him before turning back to find the boy, panicking when he couldn't immediately see him with the bundle. Running, he realised the boy had fallen asleep on the blanket, hiding him from view behind the wooden crates.

They both walked slowly back the way they had come and out into the streets around the river. The street ran in parallel to the river, the houses were large with steps up to the front door. The row was all the same with long windows either side of the door, and two further floors, though the windows to the attic rooms were small in comparison. They all had big black wooden doors so he picked the one in the middle of the row, knocking loudly on the door. It was opened quickly, as though someone had been standing waiting, by a young lady wearing a white apron and mop cap.

"I'm looking for Mrs Heggerty's establishment." Daniel looked over the girl and into the hallway. This would be out of his price range, he thought.

The maid looked them both up and down before opening the door wider to let them further into the building. "I'll get the Mrs," the girl said. "Stay there."

A very rotund woman bustled into the hallway from the door on the left. She was bedecked in jewellery, necklaces and bangles with several rings on her fingers. She was also heavily made up around her eyes and rouge on her cheeks in bright red dots. Holding out her hand to Daniel, she said, "Mrs Heggerty, Clara, I'm the proprietor of this establishment. How may I help you?"

"I'm looking for board and lodge for myself and the boy perhaps for a week until I get set on a ship. Can you tell me how much you charge?"

"This is a top establishment so my charges reflect that but you will be looked after here, sir. You didn't give me your name?" she replied.

"Sorry, Mrs Heggerty, my name is Daniel Jerrold and this is my ward also called Daniel." He pointed toward the boy who was staring at the lady.

"Please call me Clara. I don't normally take children, more trouble than some of the sailors, but I am quiet at the moment. I can let you have a room where I can put in a small bed for the boy for two shilling a night which will include breakfast for you, Mr Jerrold, and it would be a further threepence for the boy's food. If you want an evening meal, it would be a further sixpence each. Is that what you were expecting, sir?"

"Please call me Daniel. I appreciate this is a desirable establishment but that is more than I can afford especially as I may be here for some weeks. Thank you for your time." He turned, putting his hand on the boy's shoulder.

"Come now, I am sure we can come to some arrangement. As I say I am quiet at the moment. What if we say two shilling and sixpence all in and see how we go." Mrs Heggerty held out her hand again.

Daniel shook it and the deal was done. It was still much more than he wanted to pay but he remembered how expensive everything was last time he had been to London, when he had searched for Hannah. He knew he was lucky in a way as many boarding houses wouldn't take the boy, and some were not suitable, so he counted out the coins for the first night and handed them to her.

Turning to Daniel, she continued, "Evening meal will be at seven in the dining room." She pointed to the room on the other side of the hall then she waddled back into what he assumed was her sitting room, leaving them with the girl who had answered the door.

Their room was at the front of the house. Putting his bundle on the bed before placing his money pouch into the inside pocket of his jacket, he spoke to the boy. "Come on, let's go for a quick walk for some fresh air while the Miss makes up your bed. By then we will be ready for our meal."

Young Daniel was tired after the walking from the station to the docks, but he followed, saying nothing. They wandered the streets trying to get their bearings before returning for a wash before the meal.

They were served a large bowl of stew that was piping hot. There was homemade bread on the table to dip into the gravy, and both devoured every scrap. Plum duff was for afters and they both sat back in their chairs feeling completely stuffed.

Finally they retired to their room. Water had been placed in a jug to wash and fresh towels placed on the beds.

"Listen to me," Daniel said to the boy who had already changed into his nightshirt, "I will have to go to the docks tomorrow to find a ship. Will you be alright until I get back? I will be as quick as I can." He looked at the boy's crestfallen face. "We can have breakfast together then you can stay in the room."

Young Daniel nodded. He was afraid of being left on his own but wanted to prove that he wasn't a baby though he missed his aunt Adele. He wanted to cry that he didn't remember his mother and that he had always been happy where he was but said nothing. He hadn't known London was so far away so Australia must be much further and he didn't know how it would be possible to find his way home.

Young Daniel sat on the window seat watching his uncle leave the house and cross the street to the docks. He didn't want to be on his own but continued to stare at the few people going about their business. It didn't take him long to become bored so opened the door as quietly as possible with a view to finding Jane or Mrs Heggerty to talk to. Standing by the door, he listened but heard nothing, no voices, no footsteps in the hallway below.

Creeping down the stairs, trying not to make any noise himself, he sat down on the bottom step, elbows on his knees while he placed his head in his hands, just waiting. He could wait no longer so he stepped onto the tiled floor. He was careful to step only on the white tiles in a sort of game of hopscotch, where it would be bad luck to stand on the black tiles or the lines. There was no one in the dining room and he was afraid to open the door on the opposite side of the hall. Not wanting to return to the bedroom, he opened the large heavy door to the street before jumping down the steps. He knew his way to the docks and was keen to look at the ships. He could be back before anyone missed him.

No one took any notice of a young boy as he walked slowly amongst the carts and barrows. Standing next to a pile of wooden crates, he was fascinated by the hustle and bustle of men, women and children. He watched open-mouthed as one of the smaller ships lifted up the masts and sails, men running to untie ropes from the dockside. There were loud shouts to each other but he didn't understand. The ship floated on the water, silently moving out into the middle of the river. As soon as it sailed out of the dock, another seemed to appear, turning effortlessly in the middle of the river. Ropes were thrown to the still calling men who pulled the new ship to the side of the dock, fastening the ropes where the other ropes had been. Others came and went and young Daniel would have liked to have looked closer but he was afraid. He wasn't sure how long he stood watching but it seemed like hours so he decided to return to the room to wait for uncle Daniel.

Jane opened the door just as Mrs Heggerty came from the dining room.

"Hello, young Daniel. What have you been up to?" She was smiling as she seemed to float toward him.

"I've been to look at the ships," he replied.

"Well that must have made you hungry and thirsty. What about joining me for a pot of tea?"

"Yes please, Mrs Heggerty," he replied.

He was led through the other door which seemed to overflow with furniture and nick nacks on every flat surface. He would have loved to have looked more closely at the gaudy assortment of ornaments, the like he had never seen before, but thought better of it. Instead he sat right back in one of the comfortable chairs, his legs swinging. Jane brought in a tray that she placed at the table before bobbing her knee and returning to the kitchen where he could hear her talking to the cook.

Daniel returned sometime later and was shown into the lounge. "This is where you've been, young man. I hope he hasn't been any trouble, Mrs Heggerty?"

"Not at all, not at all. This young man has been telling me all about your train journey. I didn't recognise your accent but the boy said you came from Kingsmead. That's a long way to travel."

Daniel didn't want to furnish Mrs Heggerty with any more information than was necessary so changed the subject. "I've been taken on a ship but it won't be leaving for two weeks. Will that be a problem for you?"

"Not at all but what about the boy?" Mrs Heggerty looked directly at Daniel.

"I can go and look at the ships like I did today. I can do that, can't I, uncle Daniel?" the boy said brightly.

"I don't want you to be in Mrs Heggerty or Jane's way, do you hear me?" he replied. "Now thank Mrs Heggerty for your tea then you can show me where you've been today."

Young Daniel was embarrassed when Mrs Heggerty held him

to her bosom. "Oh I do miss my babies round me. Same time tomorrow, young man?" she said, releasing him.

Daniel and the boy walked back to the docks as Daniel was shown where he had stood earlier in the day. He was worried about the boy wandering about in such a strange environment but also knew he couldn't leave him locked up for the next few weeks. The boy wasn't used to freedom as Adele had kept him close to home so he was warned not to go too far from the dock entrance and under no circumstances to set foot on board a ship in case it left the dock.

For the next few weeks before they set sail Daniel was busy loading the ship with all that was needed for the long trip. He had accepted a position as a Stoker 2nd class, feeding the coal into the huge boilers to fuel the furnace to generate steam. He wasn't keen on the confined space but he had no experience on ships of this size. The wherry didn't count here. He thought the wage was good at sixteen shilling and four pence weekly until he realised he had to pay for various items. Looking at the list, candles at a farthing a week, he could get away with one between them but items like tea, sugar, butter, eggs, meat and fish he had to pay double to pay for the boy. That left him with little over ten shilling that was daylight robbery in his eyes, especially as it was hard manual work leaving him extremely tired.

Young Daniel on the other hand was having the time of his life. The first few days he stood watching what was going on before venturing closer to women sitting on upturned boxes, a number of children sitting at their feet. One of the boys came close so he asked what they were doing.

Money for old rope, the old women shouted regularly while they organised what the children had brought. Young Daniel and his new friend were given a scrap of material, and sitting cross legged, he sat watching their nimble fingers roll the rope to unravel the strands into frayed pieces. It took him much longer to complete the task, and his fingers soon became sore but he finally passed it to the woman. Taking it from him, she placed it in a bucket of smelly oil to soak overnight. His fingers and trousers were dirty but he had enjoyed his day.

As he stood to leave, his new friends asked if he would come back tomorrow and he agreed. He would have a lot to tell Daniel and Mrs Heggerty, as he walked quickly back to the lodgings.

The following morning he could hardly wait for his uncle to leave for the docks before he followed him out of the door to look for his friend who waved to him as he entered the dock gates. The boy ran to where a group of children were playing football with a stone. They suddenly headed off toward the edge of the dock as the boy in the dirty clothes looked at Daniel saying, "Going te flats te look fer old rope. There's money te be 'ad if ye find enough. De yer wanna come?"

Daniel didn't know what he meant but nodded and followed the children until they came to a set of steps. While the tide was out they could walk along the mud flats looking for rope or anything saleable. They picked up bottles, pretty stones and as many scraps of rope as they could carry. The mud tried to suck him in by his boots but he gathered what he could. "Tides comin' in," someone shouted, as they all ran back to the steps but Daniel was too late. His boots sucked him into the cloying mud. As quickly as he pulled one foot out, the other pulled him further in. Dropping the rope he'd collected, he tried to pull his foot out of his boot but it was fastened too tightly. Grabbing the lace on his left boot Daniel tried to untie it but his hands were slipping with the mud. Water was lapping around his feet, sucking him in even further. The lace knotted as he began to sob, while attempting to untie the right one. Pulling at it, Daniel fell backwards, giving him a little bit of leverage as his feet came out with a plop. The smell was something between rotting fish and sewerage which hit the back of his throat, making him want to gag.

Panicking, he shouted as loud as he could, "Help, help I'm stuck over here!" Realising that if he stood up, he would have the same problem again of his feet getting stuck so he tried calling again before crawling on his hands and knees, the water almost covering his body while trying to keep his head up. He tried to get to the fast disappearing steps but in his panic he went under, his arms flailing as he came up coughing and choking.

The boy who had befriended him earlier shouted to him, "Grab this stick, come on."

Daniel was distressed and disorientated and couldn't see where the voice was coming from. His feet no longer touched the mud as he was swirled around by the rushing tide. His head went under again, but this time someone grabbed at him pulling him up, up as he took in great gasps of air. The man threw him unceremoniously onto the top step where they both lay dripping and breathing hard. "What were ye doing, ye stupid bugger, ye could have been drowned."

Daniel couldn't answer. He began shivering as others crowded round, making way for the port polis who grabbed a piece of sailcloth to put around his shoulders. "Whose boy is this?" he asked the group who were still milling around.

"Staying at Clara's," someone shouted.

By the time Daniel heard about the commotion, the boy was ensconced in his nightshirt at Mrs Heggerty's with a blanket around him, drinking tea whilst his clothes were being washed by Jane and Hilda.

"What's happened?" Daniel said in a state.

"Don't worry, the lad's alright now. Given himself a bit of a fright and his clothes are a mess but he'll survive," Mrs Heggerty told him.

Looking at the boy he asked, "Are you alright? What were you doing?"

With that, the boy started to cry, tucking himself into the blanket.

"There, there, master Daniel, you've had a shock. Look, go and get yourself to bed while I have a chat to your uncle. Go on now." Mrs Heggerty patted him on the head.

Once he left the room Daniel asked, "What's going on? I was only gone an hour or so."

"Seems the lad ended up in the water as the tide turned too

quickly for him to get out. The polis brought him back. They may need a word with you. He was covered in slime and his boots are drying by the cooker. It's given him a shock, I'll say that." Mrs Heggerty added, "Don't be too hard on him. My lads were forever getting a soaking and it did them no harm."

"He could have been killed. How would I have explained that to his mother? I don't think he should be around the docks on his own. He's not used to it." Daniel wondered what he could do with him before saying, "Do you know where there is a second hand bookshop, perhaps I could get him some to keep him occupied, if you don't mind him staying in the room, at least for the next few days?" Daniel almost pleaded with Mrs Heggerty.

He went into the room with the intention of giving the boy a rollicking for being so stupid, but instead when he saw him asleep, his hair curling around his face, it made Daniel wonder what he had got himself into. He was no good with children. He didn't know how to talk to him, how to make sure he was safe, and more to the point he was making a mess of his own life, never mind the boy's.

The Saturday morning they took a walk to a bookshop where Daniel let the boy choose a few books, eating into yet more of his money. His idea to escape to the other side of the world wasn't working as he had imagined and at this rate he would be lucky to have any money to take to Hannah.

Daniel continued to work on the ship each day but now the boy stayed in the room if the weather was inclement, otherwise he put his coat and muffler on, sitting on the top step reading while watching his breath like a fog as the weather became colder. He no longer wanted to meet up with his new friends. He had never been so frightened in his life and the look on his uncle Daniel's face made him scared of any reprisals from that quarter. They had never been very chatty together and now the boy talked in monosyllables.

By the end of the second week, they were ready to leave. Daniel shook hands with Mrs Heggerty who then hugged the boy to her. "You'll be welcome here anytime, lad," she said. "Don't forget if you are ever in London you come and see me, make sure you do that."

He just nodded to her.

They found themselves in a bunk which seemed no bigger than a broom cupboard. Daniel had a narrow single bed while the boy had a hammock above. There was just enough room to put their belongings underneath but they had to sit on the bed in order to close the door. Food, such as it was, would be served in the galley and each of them had been given a bowl and spoon to use for every meal. In what seemed like no time at all they got into a routine where the lack of space seemed like the least of their problems.

Daniel hated the journey to Australia. The work stoking the large fire that turned the large wheel was arduous. When the wind was up, he could never find his sea legs, even struggling to sleep as the ship rolled. However he saw that the boy fit in immediately, running messages for the Captain, learning knots or helping the sailors. Within a few days, he had kicked off his boots to climb the mast to the crow's nest or to unfold the sails. As he grew in confidence as well as losing his childish looks, his name changed from young Daniel, to Danny lad, to Dan. This all made him feel very grown up as Daniel watched him grow in stature. Dan loved the feel of the sea spray on his face as he soon became one of the crew.

CHAPTER SIX
AUSTRALIA
THE REUNION

Hannah read and reread the short terse letter from Pastor John. Instead of the two or three page prose he usually wrote about the goings on in Northend, it was less than a page and straight to the point. He made it clear he was writing against Adele's wishes but his conscience had the better of him. Daniel had abandoned Adele in order to travel to Australia taking her son with him.

She couldn't speak! She knew now that God had indeed forgiven her sins. He was bringing her beloved son to her. The letter continued that they had left at the beginning of November, which meant they could be here within days. John's letter also hoped that there was no duplicity on her part, asking if she would let him know that they had arrived safely but he was torn between his duty to Adele as confidant and parishioner and as a friend to her. He felt he could no longer remain in contact with her.

Crying out loud, Hannah passed the single page to Lizzie who read it out loud to the others. Daniel, her son, would be with her soon. Her heart swelled with such happiness it threatened to overwhelm her.

Hannah heard nothing about a ship arriving but toasted in the New Year of 1874 with the hope that her son would soon be here to meet his sisters. The excitement within her was palpable but there was a matter that required her immediate attention. Since the Irishmen had been around more, Mary constantly talked about what Dennis did or said. It seemed she had been talking to him on her way home from work which was why her arrival home had become somewhat erratic. Walking together into town one Saturday morning, Hannah broached the subject. "You seem to be seeing a lot of Dennis recently. I hope you are not stopping him working?"

Mary turned pink with embarrassment as she replied, "Oh no, I see him when he is loading the cart or on his way back into town. He is very busy delivering timber to build all the new homesteads."

"Well I don't think it's a good idea to encourage him. It could give him the wrong impression and people will start talking. It could put off some suitor. I'm only thinking about your reputation, Mary." Hannah put her arm on the girl's waist.

"What reputation?" Mary laughed. "I work in a brothel, I came here on a convict ship and no man has ever looked at me. I know I'm no picture. I like Dennis and he seems to like me. If he asked me to walk out with him, I would."

"Just be careful that's all I ask. You're only a young girl, Mary, with a good heart. Don't get your head turned," Hannah stressed.

"No mam, I'll keep my virtue in my pocket." Mary laughed loudly as she left Hannah at the market setting out her goods to sell.

"Cheeky madam," Hannah laughed with her. "See you later, Miss."

Chatting to the other stallholders took Hannah's mind off Mary for a short while but she thought it might be a good idea to talk to Lizzie about her. When she told the stallholder next to her about her son coming over from England, he sent his boy to the docks to find out when the next ship was due. She was delighted to find that one should be arriving in the next two weeks if the winds were fair.

The rest of the day her thoughts were on Daniel. Her baby boy would be here for his birthday and she couldn't believe he would be ten. When she pictured him in her mind he was still the small boy she had piggy backed to Adele's before she was sent to Australia. That was the last time she had seen him, his curly hair, chubby cheeks always chattering. She couldn't picture in her mind what he would look like now.

January 17th 1874 was a day that Hannah thought she would celebrate every day for the rest of her life. Mary arrived home mid-afternoon to tell them a ship had docked the night before. The town was bustling with sailors and passengers. She agreed she would walk back into town with Hannah, who wanted to rush off straight away, waiting impatiently while the girl had a long drink of water. Lizzie agreed to look after and feed the girls, telling them there was no rush to get back. She would put them to bed if necessary.

Hannah set off at almost a run, grabbing Mary by the hand in an attempt to hurry her along. By the time they reached the edge of town, both were red faced and hot as they completed the journey in half the time. Walking with a little more decorum along the pavement, Hannah wanted to pick up her skirts and run to the docks. Walking in the shade of the buildings, passing in front of the row of shops which had sprung up over the years, the whole town seemed busy.

They passed one that was empty with one door and a small window, though blinds were hiding the interior. Above the veranda were two smaller windows. The entire wooden framework was painted a mint green which had faded badly in the heat of the sun. It was very small and seemed to have been wedged between the others either side and that was all that was keeping it upright. It was in the middle of a row of shops where the roofline was the same height, not like the ones further down the street which were all higgledy piggledy.

A breathless Mary said, "Look Hannah, wouldn't that make a lovely shop for you. You could sell goods every day!" Before Hannah could respond Mary continued, "Oh look there's Dennis. Hello Dennis, hello," she called.

Hannah was dismayed at Mary's forwardness but Dennis turned, waving to the two of them, while smiling broadly at her friend.

"Where are you going?" he asked, looking to Mary.

"We're off to the docks to see if Hannah's son has arrived on the ship," Mary replied.

"That's no place for women," Dennis responded sternly. "Give me a couple of minutes and I'll come with you."

Hannah despaired at the further delay but thought Dennis was probably right. She prayed he would hurry up.

In no time at all they were at the dock gates where Dennis told them to wait while he went to see what he could find out. Hannah paced up and down, biting the ball of her thumb.

"Isn't Dennis a kind man? Always wanting to help," Mary commented but watched as Hannah set off at a run toward a man and boy walking next to Dennis.

As Hannah got closer, she was amazed at how tall her son was but she flung her arms around him, kissing his head and face, while crying loudly. He on the other hand stood rigid as she continued to hold him to her. "Thank you, thank you for bringing him to me," she addressed Daniel but looked at her boy who looked bewildered. Hannah wasn't sure whether to hug Daniel as well but ended up holding out her hand to him while the other hand remained around her son's shoulders. "It is so good to have you home, Daniel. Your sisters are looking forward to meeting you."

"My name's Dan, everyone calls me Dan," he said, speaking for the first time.

Hannah was surprised at his gruffness but continued, "Well Dan, it's time to get your things and come home. I bet you're hungry. I can't believe you are finally here. I have missed you every day." She was shocked when he started to cry.

"Do I have to go uncle Daniel? Can't I stay on the ship with you tonight?" He moved closer to his uncle.

Daniel smiled. "How about you stay with me tonight so you can say goodbye to everyone and we can pack up your belongings. I can take you home tomorrow. That's alright, Hannah?" He almost pleaded with her.

Hannah was about to protest but Mary stepped in saying, "You've waited all this time, Hannah, one more night won't make any difference. It will give you a chance to sort out the sleeping arrangements and make a welcome home meal. Come on, come on, don't cry."

Hannah hugged her son again while Dennis arranged to pick both Daniel and Dan up the following evening. "Your carriage awaits, ladies," he said, leading them back to the dock gates. Mary put her arm round Hannah's shoulder who continued to sob while Daniel and Dan stood watching them go.

Daniel had a long talk with Dan about his mother, Hannah, explaining how much she loved him and how it was his fault she had ended up in Australia. Dan listened intently at Daniel's monologue but didn't respond. It was as though both forgot the other was there. Daniel lay on his bunk going over the meeting. He knew Hannah would be overwhelmed when she saw Dan but had expected more than a handshake. As soon as he saw her running toward them, he knew he cared for her in a way he had never cared for Adele. Her hair still had the autumnal colours though she was much slimmer than he remembered. It was with a heavy heart that Daniel regretted his impulsive decision to bring the boy to Australia. He wasn't much of a romantic but he thought Hannah would welcome him like a good friend rather than a stranger. He wanted to tell her how he felt but maybe this wasn't the right time, he mused, as he turned over to try to sleep.

The following morning, man and boy helped with the loading of the ship ready for its return trip which would be in a few days to catch the high tide. Daniel was busy shovelling coal into the hold, thankful it wouldn't be him who would be stoking the fires on the return journey. He had hated every single minute of the trip and all the money in the world couldn't persuade him to make the return journey. He had nothing to go back for but it seemed he had nothing to stay for either. In his mind he had this idea that Hannah had loved him as he did her but it seemed that wasn't to be. Perhaps he had burnt his bridges on both sides of the world, he mused.

Dan helped where he could, checking rope, folding sails while running messages for Captain Hudson when required. At then end of the day, they all shook hands, the Captain telling Daniel he was sorry to lose his stoker before turning to Dan. Passing him a single sheet of paper, he explained it was a letter of introduction should he want to join a ship when he reached the age of fourteen. Should he wish to become a sailor, he would be happy to take him under his wing. The letter would give him a passage to London to meet up where he would start his training between England and the Americas.

Daniel stared at the boy who looked as though he had been given the crown jewels such was his joy, promising to meet up as soon as he was old enough. They picked up the boy's muddle of clothes, many now too small, before heading down the gangplank.

Soon enough they were climbing on board the cart, as Dennis chatted about the seasonal high temperature and the lack of water. The horse trotted through the town which fascinated the new arrivals. The dirt road even on the main street was a deep red while the buildings were wooden, in sharp contrast to home. Home, Daniel thought, he could never go home so he no choice but to settle in this arid land.

They arrived at Hannah's house which seemed to be bursting at the seams with adults and children alike. Daniel and Dan were introduced to Mary, Adam and Lizzie Quinn as well as Amy-Rose, Kitty and young Joshua Quinn. Dennis and Daniel were invited to stay for the evening meal, which they both accepted. The conversation was stilted to begin with but again it was Dennis who seemed to have the measure of the situation, asking Mary to repeat some of the clean conversations she had heard at the hotel which had them all laughing.

Adam asked Daniel, "Will you be returning to England with the ship?"

"No fear," he replied. "One trip was enough. I never seemed to find my sea legs. When it was blowing a gale and the sails were out, I was ill at the back of the ship and when we were becalmed, my stomach was fine, but sweating in the bilges for twelve hours a day to keep the fire going wasn't my idea of fun either." He laughed as he ruffled Dan's hair. "This one was in his element from the day we set sail. You will have to ask him about his trip. It will be a different experience I can tell you."

"What will you do for work? Find something on the docks?" Adam continued, worried they would be left with another mouth to feed.

"I'd rather get as far away from the sea as I can. I get queasy just looking at the waves but I am sure I will be able to find something soon." Daniel looked at Hannah who put her head down as her face flushed.

She walked out onto the veranda to try and get her emotions in check, the joy of her son arriving and her gratitude to Daniel for bringing him threatening to overwhelm her. Turning when she heard footsteps behind her, her heart skipped a beat when she saw it was Daniel. Looking at him, she said, "I can never thank you enough for what you've done. But why after all this time?"

"That's for another time, Hannah. Look, I want you to have this." He passed her a small bag of coins. Their hands touched, both springing away as though they had been struck by lightning. "It's for Dan's keep, to help with it anyway," he said.

"I don't need your money," Hannah said more brusquely than she intended, pushing it back to him. "He's my son, my responsibility and we will manage."

Feeling rebuffed, Daniel wasn't sure what else to say. Now didn't seem like the right time to tell her how he felt. Walking past Adam, who had obviously been loitering by the door, watching them, Daniel returned to his seat next to Dan. The conversation was awkward. He didn't know what to say so was relieved when Dennis said it was time to go.

Hannah didn't look at Adam who she was sure would have heard the conversation about refusing the money. It was all he seemed to think about, though for the first time in a long time they were quite comfortable after selling the land.

As the cart was being turned, Dan rushed toward it, shouting, "Can't I come back with you until the boat sails?"

Daniel saw the fear in the boy's eyes as he replied, "Look your home is here now. I will only be on the ship another night and then I will have to find somewhere to live. I'll still see you and I'm sure your mam won't mind if you come and watch the ship sail out of the harbour. Is that alright, Hannah?"

Hannah nodded, watching him go off into the night. She placed her arm around Dan's shoulder, and although he didn't move, she knew he felt uncomfortable.

Hannah had spent the day moving beds which meant her room was very cramped. The two girls would have to share her bed while Mary was now on a single bed wedged into the corner. Dan would have to share the small middle room with Joshua who was excited at the thought of having another boy in the house.

Placing her head gently on the pillow, Hannah listened to Mary softly snoring. Amy-Rose was a restless sleeper, tossing and turning while flinging out a stray arm or leg. If Hannah turned onto her side, the little minx would roll into the warm bed space. It wasn't an ideal solution but there was little she could do about it, room anywhere in the house was at a premium but it was better than some.

She hoped to talk to Daniel, Dan, tomorrow, thinking it would probably be good to ask him about life on the ship. She didn't want him to be frightened of her but she appreciated what a wrench it must have been leaving Adele. There, she had said her name in her mind and would have to be patient if she wanted him to open up about his life with her. Once she had a place for him at the school so he could finish his education, she hoped life would settle into some kind of a pattern. There was so much to ask him and it thrilled her to think her family was together at last.

CHAPTER SEVEN

THE GOOD AND THE BAD

Life was difficult for everyone over the next few months. The dynamics in the household had changed since Dan's arrival. Although they all had their opinions, not always seeing eye to eye, there was now a tension and it was all because of Dan.

The younger children were doing well at school and encouraged to read and write when they got home. Dan hated it. He didn't want to talk about what he had done in his lessons. He didn't want to go to school, playing truant to spend his time at the dock, watching the ships being loaded or unloaded while talking to the sailors.

Hannah didn't believe it at first. After all she had walked Dan, Amy-Rose and Joshua to the school gate herself. It was her daughter who gave the game away. "Telling tales," Dan had said. When she confronted him, he just shrugged his shoulders before telling her, as he often did, that he was joining Captain Hudson as soon as he was old enough. No amount of cajoling or demanding on Hannah's part made any difference. This was the crux of her problem, the boy was adamant that he would become a sailor as soon as he was fourteen and go back to England and there was nothing she could do about it. Her hope was that the longer he lived with them, the urge to leave would fade.

Adam thought she was too soft, telling her that if Dan wasn't going to school he could work in the garden, chop wood and gather water, none of which he was currently inclined to do. Hannah found it hard to accept that this sullen child was indeed the cheerful, chatty boy she had left behind all those years ago. Daniel had told her that Adele mollycoddled him, he was used to being the centre of her world. Give him time, he told her, but life didn't seem to be getting any better and it was putting a strain on Hannah's friendship with Lizzie who sided with her husband. Hannah was beginning to despair.

Hannah sat next to Dan on the veranda steps. Her arm went around him as she kissed the top of his head. He still stiffened at her touch but the look of terror in his eyes was no longer there. Taking a deep breath, Hannah began. "You know when I first came here, I wanted to lay on my bed and cry. I hated it, I missed you every day but couldn't see a way to ever get back to you."

Dan looked at her briefly before putting his head down again.

"What got me through was my friends. Mary told me I had to be strong if I ever wanted to see you again. I didn't want you to think I had abandoned you so I wrote to you hoping you would reply when you were older."

"I never got a letter," Dan said gruffly.

"Well I always put a letter in for you when I wrote to Daniel, but no matter, you're here now and all I want is for you to be happy." Hannah was disturbed that Dan had never received her letters and had an idea Adele might have had something to do with that but didn't want to say and alienate her son any further.

"I know you miss everyone at home. I did, but you can make friends here, if you try." She really didn't know what else to say so was surprised when Dan spoke.

"What happened to my dad?"

"Your dad?" What could she say, certainly not that he was a rapist and a drunkard. "He died before you were born. I'm sure he would have loved you as much as I do," Hannah lied.

"What happened?" Dan asked.

This wasn't the conversation she had expected, but it was at least a conversation and not monosyllables but she owed him an explanation.

"He was much older than me and when he died, his family threw me out. There was no room at my parents so I headed for Kingsmead to find work. That's how I met uncle Daniel. He was travelling in that direction and agreed to give me a lift. I was lucky to be taken in by Annie, and Northend became my family and yours."

"Uncle Daniel said you were sent here because of him. He said it was his fault so why are you still friends?" Dan asked.

"Well, he helped me out when I needed it so when he asked for money to pay his fine, I willingly went to the gaol but was accused of stealing a ring and sent here. I had no chance to get you. I was distraught." Hannah shivered at the thought.

"Is that why you left me with aunt Adele?"

"Yes, I thought I would only be gone a few hours, and I'm still friends with Daniel because he brought me the greatest gift of all, you." Hannah pulled her son closer to her. "Will you try and be friends with everyone? Maybe then you will feel happier being here with people who love you," Hannah told him.

Dan stood. "I'll try." As he walked away, he continued, "But I'm still going to become a sailor."

The words came like a kick in the stomach. It was the longest conversation they'd had, the closest they had been since he arrived. She had tried to be honest with him but it was going to be an uphill battle to get him to change his mind.

Strangely Dan talked to Dennis and Mary and it was the two of them who brokered a truce in the household. Eventually Hannah, Dan, Dennis, Mary and Daniel sat round the kitchen discussing the boy's options. The deal, which Dan had to agree to, was that he would attend school to get his certificate and also be in charge of collecting water each morning and chop wood each evening during the week. In return Dennis would employ him to help at the timber yard, loading and unloading the cart on a Saturday for which he would pay him sixpence. Hannah felt that this would be coming out of Dennis' own pocket but said nothing. Daniel would collect him to take him fishing early each Sunday morning. Dan agreed readily though Hannah stipulated that should he play truant the whole agreement would end.

For a few further months, the deal seemed to work well and harmony of a kind returned to the house. Daniel called to see them unexpectedly one evening to inform them that he was going to work on the railway, his time at the docks over for now. He had never enjoyed being close to the sea and they were looking for gangs of men to work in the north, digging a route through the outback for the railway. He wasn't sure when he would be back, though as the line came closer they would see more of him. He left his fishing rod for Dan to look after before shaking hands with everyone. Before taking his leave, he passed a letter to Hannah to read when he was gone. They all stood at the side of the road watching him go back toward town but he didn't look back.

The letter sat on the kitchen table while Hannah got the girls ready for bed and settled. It was Lizzie who said, "Come on, Hannah, don't leave us in suspense. Put us out of our misery and open the letter."

She was nervous and excited at the same time, wondering what it would say. Reading it, Hannah was surprised at Daniel's honesty but was more surprised at the land registry paperwork with it. Daniel had purchased the small shop on Market Street but had put it in both his and Hannah's names. He explained in the letter that this was in case anything happened to him while he was away. The front room could be turned into a small shop while the first floor held two small bedrooms. He had already spoken to Dennis and Mary who would move into the rooms above once they were married. The rest was a sort of love letter. Her heart skipped a beat by his thoughtfulness but she tried to compose herself to ask, "Did you know about this, Mary?"

"Yes, Daniel talked to Dennis about it. In fact I have the keys." She took them out of her pocket and passed them to Hannah. "He wanted to buy something before he went away because he knew property would increase in price once the railway arrived, but he also wanted you to have some security. As he said, he has no one to leave anything to and has always looked on Dan as family. That's not all he wrote, is it?" She laughed at Hannah.

"No, it's not but I am not going to read out his ramblings. They are for me alone," Hannah said, somewhat embarrassed.

It was much later when the house was quiet that Hannah took the lamp out onto the veranda, sitting on the steps to read properly what Daniel had written. She was surprised. Although she knew he cared for her, she hadn't realised just how much. His writing was childlike in a way but the sentiment was touching. Her heart beat faster at the thought of the two of them getting close.

He told her he thought he had fallen in love with her the first day they met although he didn't realise it at the time. He admired her determination in wanting to provide for her child, and wrote that he should have taken her away when he saw her in Kingsmead with her new son. Did she remember the day she had gone to register his birth, when she was distraught? He had wanted to put his arms around her then, to tell her that it would be alright. He should have spoken up but he was a coward. She had her life and he had his. He knew that she loved her husband, Mickey, and perhaps it was too soon to think of anyone in that way but he felt he had to say something before he went away. He would never return to England and he finished the letter by saying that sometime in the future he hoped they could become more than friends. If she could think about it while he was away, that was all he asked.

Smiling as she folded the letter, Hannah took herself off to bed. He had given her a lifeline again giving her the shop and she would make it a success for her and her children. She felt somehow content. Daniel would always look out for her and for that she was grateful. As for becoming more than friends, he was right, it was much too early for her to think about another relationship, but she knew she cared deeply for him, hoping this would be enough for now.

After dropping the children at the school gates, Hannah went along to the small row of buildings. Opening the door into the room that was to become her shop, she felt the gossamer of spiders' webs like silk against her cheek. The room was dusty as was the stone floor.

The small kitchen at the back had stairs to two small rooms which would be made into bedrooms. It would be difficult to get a double bed into either room but she thought Mary would be happy once the place had been cleaned up.

Rolling up her sleeves, Hannah opened the kitchen door leading to a communal yard where she found a cold water tap, and filling up her bucket, she set about cleaning the place. It didn't take her long as there was no furniture to move but she soon became hot, opening the front door to let a breeze flow through. The small stove, once she had wiped the dust away, looked serviceable but she had no wood to light it. She would leave that in Dennis' capable hands.

Over the next few days, she bought various items to sell though she had nothing to sit them on, nor did she have anywhere to place her money other than her dress pocket. The shop soon became a meeting place for the other stallholders who were pleased she could now trade every day. The daily market bustled with the increasing number of people living in the town. It was a community supporting each other, something Hannah felt very much a part of.

Far from living in a backwater now people had moved out in all directions as they claimed land from the outback to build their homesteads. The creaking wagons pulled by snorting horses as men called out now peppered the silence. Small settlements seemed to have moved in all around them. They were no longer at the end of the road but somewhere in the middle. There were row upon row of tiny basic clapboard shacks, some nothing more than four walls and a roof sitting on a small plot. Everything happened in the one room, eating, sleeping, cooking, making and producing babies while ragged children played barefoot in the dirt.

Those with a bit more money built bigger homes with one large room come kitchen with a bedroom either side. They were long and thin taking up much of the frontage, and some were fortunate enough to be able to build a veranda to give some shade and make them look more permanent.

Compared to many in the area, Hannah and her friends seemed comparatively well off. Not only did they have a regular income from Adam, Mary as well as Hannah, but their garden was filled with vegetables thanks in the main to Adam and Dennis as well as Joshua when he wasn't shadowing Dan.

The outback was being pushed further and further back, trees felled making the area a large suburb of the town. Gone was the relative solitude that Hannah craved since Mickey's death. Gone too was part of the convict factory; those now coming to Cheapside did so of their own free will. The remaining building became a prison.

Hannah bought many items from the correction facility that she thought she would be able to sell on. She picked up anything from bedding to bowls, cutlery to crockery, anything she thought would turn a profit. There were a number of small tables which she used in the shop, and she even bought bunk beds for the growing children, laughing at the thought that they may have been the ones her and Mary had slept in when they first arrived. That seemed another life, as did her life in England though when Daniel first arrived she was reminded of how they first met.

Each day Hannah walked into the town with the children, leaving Kitty with Lizzie who had now produced a daughter, Victoria, who was the apple of Adam's eye. Mary was still working at the hotel trying to save money for when she married Dennis. He was a kind and thoughtful man who thought the world of Mary, and Hannah had warmed to him. Although much older than Mary it didn't seem to matter to either of them.

Hannah hadn't seen or heard from Daniel since he went to work on the railway line miles away. Eventually the men would return home as the line got closer to Cheapside but she had no idea how long that would be. The railway station was proposed for the land where the factory had been though there was talk of running a freight line when the new harbour was built.

Hannah was happy enough helping Mary to make her wedding dress. Nothing plain for Mary, she wanted lace, ribbons and furbelow around the hem.

Hannah suggested, "Why don't we do something with your Sunday bonnet? I could sew flowers around the brim?"

This was met with disdain by Mary. "I want new. I'm only getting married the once, so no, it won't do. You know I've been saving money so come on, let's have another look in the haberdashery."

Hannah sighed but Mrs Coyle, the shopkeeper, sighed even louder when she again brought out the boxes with ribbon, lace and material for Mary to root through. "Ain't got no new stock since you were last in," she said sarcastically.

This didn't put Mary off, her fingers feeling the goods before saying to Hannah for the umpteenth time, "Dennis said to have what I want. If I need money, he'll let me have some. He's such a kind man."

Hannah almost said the last words with Mary, she had heard them at least a hundred times. In Mary's eyes, he was a saint, though he was the lucky one.

Mary picked up a number of ribbons to show Hannah.

"You can't put those colours together, Mary, you'll look as though you work in a bordello. No, look at these."

May laughed. "Well I do, but not in the way you mean, anyway I want bright, cheerful colours so humour me."

CHAPTER EIGHT
THE WEDDING

"Come on, girls, let's have you washed and ready for bed," Hannah said to Amy-Rose, Kitty and Victoria.

"It's too early," Amy-Rose stated.

"Don't start, madam, we've got a lot to do for Mary's big day so come here while I give your hands and face a lick."

"We'll go into the garden out of your way," Adam said before nodding to Dan and Joshua to join him.

Once the water was hot enough, Hannah took the pans into the room to fill the tin bath. "Can I wash your hair? I'd like to."

"If it makes you happy then you can though I'm not a girl anymore," Mary replied.

"No, you will soon be a married woman but you will always be a sister to me." Hannah joined in the squealing as she poured the water over Mary's hair. Gently rubbing the soap into the girl's hair, Hannah was so grateful to Mary for helping her. She was always a voice of reason even for her young age. She realised how much she would miss her when she moved out of the house. Leaving her to wash and dry herself, Hannah busied herself cutting material into rags to put in Mary's hair.

"I hope these rags will give a bit of curl to your poker straight hair but you'll have to sleep in them," Hannah said, winding the wet hair around the rag in turn.

"I don't care how uncomfortable they are to sleep in, I want to look my best," Mary told her.

"And you will look beautiful, radiant in fact." Hannah hugged her friend, both trying not to cry.

The morning of the wedding was all hustle and bustle in the house as everyone seemed to get in each others' way. Hannah became melancholy when she thought that the number in the overcrowded house would be one less after today.

The timber yard horse and cart had been washed and cleaned the day before by both Dennis and Dan, the seat covered in a white sheet with garlands of greenery either side. The surprise was Daniel had managed to get to town for the wedding so became driver for the day. Adam had been overwhelmed when Mary asked him to give her away. Dan wasn't quite so enthusiastic when Dennis asked him to be best man. Hannah as ever was grateful to Dennis for his attempt to include her son in everything.

Hannah and Lizzie had offered to make the wedding breakfast at the house but Mary wanted them both to enjoy the day so organised the reception at the hotel. Mary looked delightful in a pale grey dress that had a bright blue ribbon along the hemline and a sash of the same colour at the waist that tied in a bow at the back. She had wanted the blue ribbon on her bonnet but Hannah managed to dissuade her telling her it would make her look too pale. Her skin was still marked, though as she grew older they had faded. Apparently, she told Hannah, as a child she had some kind of pox which hadn't been treated, leaving the marks.

Lizzie made her a beautiful posy of flowers from the garden, some probably weeds, but they were colourful and Mary was delighted. The white lace gloves that belonged to Hannah finished off the extravagant attire and Mary looked lovely. They all climbed onto the cart for a trip to the church where the couple would become man and wife.

The ladies from the hotel were outside the church when the cart arrived all in a range of loud coloured dresses that hardly covered their breasts but they didn't seem to mind. The owner was wearing the largest hat Hannah had ever seen. They were grouped together talking loudly oohing and aahring as Mary was helped off the cart.

Mr and Mrs O'Reilly came out of the church to rapturous applause. It seemed half the town had come out to see them. Mary said something to Dennis and they both moved down the path that led to the graveyard where they placed her posy on Mickey's grave. Hannah cried, thinking what a marvellous couple they were. The whole day was wonderful and Mary and Dennis looked so happy. Hannah thought it must be marvellous to marry for love, thinking her first marriage had been a disaster. Although she had grown to love Mickey, she knew in the beginning it was a marriage of convenience for her. Still she was happy for her friend, her sister.

The hotel had put long tables in the smaller room for the wedding breakfast that were overflowing with food while Dennis had paid for numerous barrels of ale to be placed behind the bar.

Day went into early evening and while drink was flowing, the band the Irish had put together started up. This was the part of the day Hannah was dreading so she said she would take the children home, they had seen enough excitement for one day. Kitty and Victoria were already tired, though Amy-Rose wanted to stay. Joshua was hanging on Dan's every word, sitting with some of the men and neither wanted to leave either. Hannah heard her son join in the banter, giving as good as he got, seemingly at ease in the men's company. He was certainly happier in their company than hers, she realised unhappily.

In the end Lizzie and Adam said they would take the children. Amy-Rose was set to have a tantrum, saying it wasn't fair, she wasn't a baby, but Hannah was adamant that she didn't want her to be around as the drink continued to flow. Hannah agreed she would walk back with Dan in an hour or so but felt a little lost when they left. She stood watching Mary socialising with the guests, smiling widely as she caught Dennis' eye. She thought back to the scruffy street urchin who had helped her on that terrible journey by ship to Australia. Mary always said she would make something of herself and now she had.

The guests were having a wonderful time, and the Irish mingled with the ladies from the hotel as they all drank copious amounts of alcohol. They were laughing, talking and dancing. The women had started dancing, grabbing any available man going around the floor in a quick jig. They whooped and hollered as they sped around the dance floor. Dresses in purple, red, blue and green spun round, giving a kaleidoscope of colours, making Hannah feel quite dizzy. The men swung the women in all directions as the music continued faster and faster. Not a drop of drink had passed Hannah's lips even when they proposed a toast to the happy couple. She admired the women in a way, really she did, but she just couldn't. It made her somewhat aloof from the others, starchy, and a feeling that she always stood on the edge of any merriment. Even so, she felt her foot tapping to the music as she stood at the side of the dance floor just watching the proceedings.

Someone grabbed her around the waist. Turning, she saw it was Samuel Fletcher and as she tried to pull away, he pushed her back against the wall so she couldn't move. She hadn't seen him for some time and hoped he had gone away. In her panic, her hair got caught around one of his shirt buttons but she yanked at it, pulling it out at her scalp. She fell toward a chair but he put his hand out and his arm around her shoulders. No one noticed her fear.

"Leave me alone," she hissed, "I don't want anything to do with you. Let me go."

Ignoring her outburst, he said, "I'm not much of a dancer but we could do a turn around the room." He forced her to her feet.

He held her too tightly as Hannah struggled to get away but the harder she struggled, the tighter he held her. They were crashing into other dancers as he laughed at her. "Yer not afraid of me, Mrs Phelan, are ye?" He stressed her name. "We go back a long way you and me. Let's do a dance to toast those we've left behind, you know who I mean?"

The music continued as they moved uncomfortably in and out of the other dancers. Hannah didn't want to make a scene and spoil Mary's day but she had to extract herself from this terrible man's arms somehow. She could smell the drink on his breath, as he staggered. She managed to push him away, running through the other dancers but ended by the back door to the yard. It wasn't the best place to be alone but she felt sick as she tried to get her breath.

Moving into the shadows so she couldn't be seen but she could watch the door in case that man came looking for her.

She couldn't face going back into the main room to get Dan but she couldn't go home without him. What a mess. Why did things always happen to stop her from being happy? Realising someone was now stood in the doorway, she became afraid, very afraid, trying not to move. Her terror turned to delight when she realised it was Daniel. Moving out of the shadows, he looked directly at her.

"What are you doing out here on your own?" he asked.

"I'm not on my own now you are here." Hannah tried to laugh but cried out instead.

"Hey, come on, Hannah, why do I always seem to make you cry? Weddings have the same effect on me. Come on, please don't cry. I'm no good when women cry, you know that." He held his arms out and she fell into them as she continued to sob.

She wanted him to hold her to make her safe so she told him about Samuel Fletcher and what he had said to her. Daniel listened, not interrupting until she had finished. "You do get yourself into some scrapes, Hannah, don't you, but don't worry it will be sorted just leave it with me." Hannah went to speak but he stopped her. "Don't ask any questions. He won't bother you again. Now come on, let's go back into the festivities." He took her hand and reluctantly Hannah returned to the room where the noise seemed to have got louder if that were possible.

Hannah and Daniel took to the dance floor somewhat uncomfortably, arms holding gently. Both were waltzing in step around their emotions to the same music, knowing how they felt but not sure what to do about it. As his hand brushed hers, an overwhelming frisson shuddered through her body. She wanted to hide in his strong arms forever, where she felt safe.

For Daniel, he had the irresistible urge to pull her even closer, to breathe in her scent before kissing her but he didn't. He didn't want to spoil the moment while he felt her relax into him as they swayed to the music as though they were the only people in the room. Their feet shuffled around the dance floor, both thinking that this was a most wonderful feeling.

As the band stopped, the two of them sprang apart uncomfortably though Hannah didn't remove her hand from his. She heard him whisper her name and her heart skipped a beat. This couldn't happen, not now, not today or tomorrow. It was still too soon.

Hannah waited until Mary and Dennis left the nuptials, hugging the girl tightly to her, both in tears of pure joy. They were adjourning to rooms above the timber yard that they had cleaned and furnished over the last few months. Although Daniel had offered them the rooms above the shop, they felt they wanted to start out on their own.

"I'll see you tomorrow," Mary said to Hannah.

"No you won't, Mrs O'Reilly, you've got a husband to look after now." Hannah laughed, pushing her toward Dennis.

Hannah and Daniel walked back into the hotel to look for Dan who she found almost falling asleep on a chair. He didn't want to walk all the way home even when Daniel offered to walk with them, and the truth was neither did Hannah. Her shoes were crippling her, her feet were paining and all she wanted was to be tucked up in her bed.

She was surprised when Daniel suggested they stay in his rooms. It made sense, he said. Hannah could have the bed and he would share the spare room with Dan if she had any blankets in the shop. Hannah readily agreed.

They had to walk the long way round to the back of the shop as Hannah's keys were at home and Daniel only had the key to the back door. He quickly lit a lamp so they could look for bedding while Dan sat half asleep on the stairs. Hannah could feel Daniel looking at her in the shadow of the light but tried not to smile. After sorting bedding and placing it on the floor for Dan, she told him to fold his Sunday clothes neatly before leaving the remaining bedding for Daniel. In the light from the lamp, she watched him slowly climb up the stairs toward her. The small landing gave them no room to pass each other but Daniel stopped two steps from the top so that his face was level with hers.

She knew he wanted to kiss her but the look in her eyes stopped him.

"Not yet," she said before turning and going into the bedroom leaving him standing on the stairs.

Sitting on the bed, Hannah removed her shoes and stockings, rubbing her aching feet. Her dress she hung on the back of the chair that was the only other piece of furniture in the room other than the bed. It was sparse though in reality there was no room to put anything else even a chest of drawers so Daniel's clothes were under the chair. As she lay almost on the point of sleep, she thought of Daniel. She could smell him on the bedding. She cared for him, she knew that. She was eternally grateful to him for bringing her son to her. She also realised that he really did love her and she could love him but it couldn't be. The crux of it was he was still married and there was no way round that. She couldn't, wouldn't live in sin.

Daniel lay on the floor in the other room, listening to Dan sleeping deeply. Hannah had said not yet, not no, not never but not yet. However long it took, he would wait.

The following morning neither of them commented about the night before. Hannah got herself ready to go to church leaving Dan still in his bed. He would go fishing with Daniel if he got up but she would see them both at lunch. Being alone with Lizzie on the walk home would give her a chance to explain her whereabouts and talk about the wedding.

Lizzie laughed loudly when Hannah told her they had stayed at Daniel's, commenting that they were made for each other and that was no disrespect to Mickey. She deserved to be happy so what was stopping her?

Hannah said just two words. "His wife."

Hannah felt a little embarrassed when Daniel turned up for lunch with Dan and was afraid to speak to him directly in case her feeling became obvious. Fortunately they had plenty to say about the wedding and what an incredible day it had been. They all agreed that Mary would be missed in the household though she wasn't too far away. Adam stopped the conversation dead when he looked directly at Hannah asking if she had seen her friend Mr Fletcher in the bar. She picked up the plates, trying to bustle about so she didn't have to answer, knowing he was goading her to respond in front of Daniel.

As Daniel stood to take his leave, he looked directly at Hannah though addressed them all when he told them he would be home more often as the work on the railway was finishing, though he couldn't be specific as to exactly when. Dan followed them out, standing beside Hannah who put her arm around his shoulder. They stood close together watching until Daniel was a speck at the bottom of the road into town. Hannah was relieved that they hadn't had any time alone as her feelings were getting the better of her.

Life for Hannah had become a routine of opening the shop six days a week, which she enjoyed. Mary had given up her job in the hotel, now she was married, so called in to see her most days. She looked after the shop when Hannah went off to auctions or house sales. Business was booming as people came in to sell all sorts of items they no longer needed or were desperate for money. Hannah had to make a sign for the door stating she wasn't a pawn shop, the memories of that awful man in Stainsby coming to mind, the man with the ill fitting wig. It was his fault she was in Australia.

Sailors would quite often call in with items they had acquired on their travels. Hannah didn't ask whether they had been purchased legitimately, stolen or gambled. It wasn't her nature to quiz her customers. Many wanted money to buy ale while they were ashore and although she didn't agree with where they spent their money, she wouldn't have a business if she was too particular. One piece which took Hannah's fancy was a carved ivory coloured wooden box which had a lock but no key. The sailor said he had bought it at a market in Africa and showed strange carved animals, lion, giraffe and elephant. They bartered over it for a while but Hannah thought it would make a good present for Dan's birthday. He could put in his letter from Captain Hudson as well as any monies he saved.

She tried opening the box with a knife but was afraid to use too much force in case she damaged it. Hannah hoped Dennis would be able to make some kind of key for it giving it to Mary to take home. A few days later it was brought back with a key made from a piece of metal bent into shape. She was a little disappointed when she opened it to find the box was empty.

Daniel had only returned to town on a couple of occasions since the wedding for which she was thankful in a way as it didn't give them chance to talk about their feelings. She wasn't sure what she could say to him. Yes, she enjoyed his company. He made them all laugh when he talked about his escapades on the railway. Most important of all, yes, she loved him, there it was in plain sight, she loved him, hoping one day they would be together but there was no rush. She had enough to think about trying to make ends meet and bring up her family.

She loved him for always making a fuss of Dan, trying to convince him that Australia was the land of opportunity but he was still as determined to join a ship as the day he arrived. Hannah thought, no hoped, that if she didn't talk to Dan about it, it would never happen but Daniel often talked to him about their time aboard the ship.

Desperation made her try to talk to him about his determination to become a sailor again but it was difficult for her not to lose her temper with him.

"You know I don't want you to go, I couldn't bear to lose you again." She took his hand in hers but he pulled away.

"I've done what you asked and tried to be happy but I'm not. The only time I was really happy was with aunt Adele and on the ship," Dan said.

Trying to choke back the tears, Hannah looked at her boy who had grown so much over the last four years and in a way she admired him for never wavering in his dreams but she just couldn't lose him again. "What will it take for you to stay? Please Dan, I don't want you to go."

He didn't speak and that made it worse for Hannah. She hadn't lost him, she had never really had him. If she didn't give her blessing, he would just run away, she was sure and she couldn't keep him locked up. Bit by bit her heart shattered as she walked into the garden, tears falling unabated down her cheeks.

The tension in the house became almost unbearable for both of them as they were both determined to get their way on the matter, though deep down Hannah knew she had lost.

In what seemed like a blink of an eye for Hannah, she began preparations for Dan's fourteenth birthday, the day she had been dreading. He didn't want a fuss, he just wanted to leave school and find a ship to take him to England where he would wait for Captain Hudson.

In the end, Hannah, Dennis and Dan talked in the shop away from the others, especially Amy-Rose who was very resentful of Dan and what she saw as favouritism on Hannah's part. She was now eight and certainly had plenty to say on the subject even that she would be glad when Dan left. Hannah had grabbed her arm, telling her to apologise to her brother but she had refused. She didn't cry, just became more angry and in the end Hannah had sent her to her room for defiance.

It was when Hannah was talking to Mary about Dan that Dennis became the calming influence once again. Dennis offered to take him on full time as an apprentice at the timber yard but Dan was having none of it so a compromise was reached. Dennis said he could work at the yard until Daniel came back. Then and only then could he go to the docks to find a ship with Daniel making sure that everything would be alright for the boy.

Dan wasn't happy, he just wanted to set sail on the first ship leaving, but he reluctantly agreed, but not for too long, he added.

Hannah felt she had been given some breathing space to try and get her son to change his mind, though she hadn't in the last four years so a few weeks probably wouldn't make any difference. She realised she would have to let him go with her blessing otherwise she would lose him forever, thinking she had lost him once and couldn't bear to lose him again but if she agreed, he might at least write to her so she would know he was safe.

CHAPTER NINE
MAKING DECISIONS

It was the middle of May 1878 before Daniel returned to Cheapside. The bulk of the work on the railway was finished ready to lay the remaining track that would bring trains right into the centre of town. Part of the old convict facility had been turned into a station while the rest remained as the central prison.

He agreed he would be happy to take Dan along to the dock to talk to the captains to find a suitable ship to take him back to England. He would meet him after he finished his work with Dennis so he didn't have the long walk home and back.

Daniel hadn't seen Dan for a while so was surprised how he had filled out working for Dennis, his face losing its childlike features. While he wasn't yet a man, he had grown into a fine boy, tall with broad shoulders from all the lifting of the wood at the timber yard.

They walked to the dock side by side, Dan clutching his letter from Captain Hudson, talking animatedly about his chance to sail away. The two of them laughed loudly as Daniel reminded him about his own feelings on the journey which had been traumatic to say the least and he didn't envy Dan one bit.

The port had increased in size over the last four years, goods brought here to transport all over Western Australia. There were a number of ships anchored off, waiting for a berth so they could be unloaded once there was room on the small jetty. Daniel spoke to a number of men who were working along the dockside to find out which ships were ready to sail. Most seemed in agreement that the schooner at the end of the jetty was probably the best ship for the boy. It was about the same size as the one they travelled to Australia in but was powered by sail only having more than one mast with rigging fore and aft.

The two of them climbed the gangplank to seek out the captain who spoke at length to Daniel before asking for the letter of introduction from Dan. The latter held his breath as the captain scrutinised it before patting him on the shoulder. He told them both that they would be sailing on the early evening tide in three days' time so he expected Dan to be there in good time. The ship would be returning to England via South Africa where they would be loading the ship. While it was relatively empty, part of Dan's job would be to swab out the decks, scrubbing and cleaning for which he would be paid a small wage. Dan didn't ask how much. He didn't care, he just wanted to set sail.

Hannah was bereft when they returned, realising Dan would be leaving in a few days but for the first time since he had arrived in Australia she could see the happiness in his eyes. He talked non-stop to the ever-eager Joshua about what he was going to do and the younger boy hung on his every word. She spent the next few days with high emotions that threatened her very being. She couldn't bear to let her son go while knowing that he had never been happy so she tried her best not to become too tearful when he was around. Much of her evenings were spent altering Dan's clothes, lengthening his trousers, moving buttons on his shirt and darning socks. She gave him the long bag she had been given when she arrived in Australia. It was made out of strong bleached calico and fit nicely under his hammock. His wooden box could be placed safely in the bottom with his clothes on the top. Daniel had given him a cord to put the key on so it would be safe around his neck.

All too soon, the day arrived with everyone going with Dan to the ship and though he would have preferred a smaller entourage, he said nothing. Seeming older than his years, he shook hands with Adam, Lizzie and Dennis who grabbed him in a bear hug. Mary joined in, telling Dan how much she would miss him before he stood in front of Hannah. She hugged him tightly as though her life depended on it until he began coughing. Daniel put a hand on his shoulder to lead him up the gangplank as Joshua shouted, asking him to write to him about his adventures.

Dan didn't turn. He walked quickly until he was out of sight. Then he was gone.

Hannah had been holding her breath, trying not to cry, hoping he would run back to her but only Daniel returned. The floodgates opened as Mary grabbed her to stop her falling. Lizzie passed Victoria to Adam and the three women held each other, crying together.

Daniel stood beside Dennis, watching the gangplank being raised and the ropes dragged onto the deck. Slowly and majestically, the small schooner moved away from the jetty, turning behind one of the other ships so it could head out of the harbour and out into the open ocean.

Surprising everyone, Hannah turned and ran as though she was on fire toward the dock gates. The others were slow to react as she turned out of sight. Running past the startled horse and cart, Hannah continued on the main road past the shop until she came to the waste ground heading uphill. The limestone hill where the Round House stood had the best view over the harbour and she headed in that direction without slowing. The Union Flag was still flying outside the building which doubled as a lookout post and small prison having only had eight cells. Arthur's Head was at the top of the hill where Hannah knew she would be able to watch the ship until it became a small dot on the ocean.

Struggling to breathe when she reached the top, she stood gasping, watching the schooner sailing further and further away, watching the sea spray as it rose and fell like a symphony in tune to her beating heart. Putting her hand up above her eyes, she scoured the ship for any sign of Dan but could see no one. The ship ploughed a white ribbon spreading out from the stern in the azure blue sea that grew longer as the ship sailed on. The ribbon drifted toward the coastline, mingling with the waves as it dispersed onto the beach. Hannah wanted to reach out and grab the ribbon to pull the ship back toward her to bring her boy back home.

How long she stood there, she didn't know, standing motionless until she felt someone moving slowly toward her. It was Daniel, she knew it would be him, but at this moment in time she just wanted to be left alone in her grief so she continued to look out to sea. He didn't speak for which she was grateful. The schooner eventually slipped over the horizon toward the now setting sun whereby Hannah flopped to the ground. Daniel thought she was going to topple over the cliff face so he grabbed her to him, his arms remaining around her.

For a short moment Hannah placed her head against his shoulder before sitting upright saying, "That's it then, I've lost my son again. Before I always had hope that one day I would see him again but now he is lost to me forever. I could never make him happy. Me his mother, I failed him. What does that make me?"

"Hannah, he has gone with your blessing which is a good thing and he knows you love him," Daniel said quietly. "He'll come back to you one day with a ship of his own, mark my words."

"I'm worried about him being in London on his own with no one to look after him, he's only a child," Hannah sobbed.

"No, he won't be alone. I told him to go and see Mrs Heggerty and Jane. They will look out for him. He's a sensible lad." Daniel pulled her closer to him. He wanted to take the pained look away from her but he knew he couldn't, how could he? Standing, he said, "Come on, let's get you home." He held out his hand to help her up. They walked down the hill hand in hand, both wanting that closeness but for very different reasons.

They reached the bottom just as the light was beginning to fade. Dennis and Mary were waiting for them. They had taken the others home before returning to wait for Hannah and Daniel, deciding they would wait however long it took. Mary watched them walking close together holding hands. "About time," she said to Dennis who hugged his wife to him.

Hannah couldn't speak but was grateful to her friends. Tomorrow is another day, she thought, my girls are still here, my life has to go on for their sake. Perhaps now her beautiful son would be happy as he had never been happy with her in Australia. That was a fact and she would have to live with it. She had told him she would welcome him back with open arms but deep down she knew that would never happen. The best she could hope for would be letters or a return one day with a ship of his own. That night she prayed to God for Dan to have a safe journey and to be happy, always happy.

The household returned to some sort of order and the only person she could really talk to about Dan was Joshua who missed him almost as much as her. Each day he would ask where they thought Dan would be and each day the answer was she didn't know.

Hannah still walked into town each day, dropping Amy-Rose and Joshua at school and within weeks Kitty would be joining them. Where had all those years gone, she often thought when they had first bought the house and land. She thought she was somebody then, a wife then a mother but now she hated walking home each evening. There were so many shacks on the road home that she never felt comfortable walking past, especially on her own each Saturday. Men would stand in their doorways eyeing her as she went on her way. Children would often throw stones as she pulled the bogey along but she said nothing. If she mentioned it to Lizzie and Adam, he would insist on walking into town to meet her, she was sure, but he had enough trying to keep the garden going.

She wished she could sell her share of the property and move into town but knew her friends wouldn't be able to buy her out. They all still had money from the sale of the land which was put away for a rainy day, while Adam's wages and Hannah's money from the shop kept them from poverty but only just.

A further three months went by, turning what had been an extremely dry winter into spring. There had been no rain for a long time and the stream at the bottom of the land was now no more than a trickle. Hannah thought it might be a good idea to bring a container for water from town each time she took the bogey to the shop.

She was still thinking about it when Mary bustled into the shop, not waiting to shut the door before saying loudly, "Oh Hannah, I've got some great news."

Hannah didn't give the girl chance to finish as she saw a letter in her hand. Snatching it from her, Hannah was disappointed when she realised it was from Pastor John and not Dan. Reading it quickly, there were tears in her eyes when she turned to Mary. "It's not from Dan but John. He says Dan had to wait a month to meet up with the Captain so went to stay with Adele. He has been to Northend to see everyone who were all delighted to see him. He travelled on the train by himself all the way to Kingsmead."

Mary laughed. "Well, didn't he get all the way to London on his own? At least we know he is safe and well." They talked for a little longer about the letter until Mary could wait no longer. "You haven't asked about my great news, Hannah."

Looking puzzled, Hannah replied, "Sorry I thought the letter was the news."

"It's not all about you, Hannah. The rest of us have a life as well, you know, so go on ask me what my great news is."

"Come on, Mrs O'Reilly don't keep me in suspense." Hannah tried to smile at the girl.

"I'm going to have a babby. My own. Can you believe that?"

Hannah grabbed the girl to her, hugging her tightly as they laughed together. "That's the most wonderful news, Mary, it really is. What does Dennis think?"

"He's made up, walking round like cock of the walk, I tell you. We can't believe how happy we are."

Hannah knew she would have to put all thoughts of her son and the letter to the back of her mind and give her best friend her day in the sun. Mary talked and talked about this wondrous happening as though she was the first woman ever to fall pregnant. She almost tutted if anyone came into the shop to put her off her stride. Eventually Hannah could take no more, sending Mary into the kitchen to make some tea.

The children came into the shop after school so Mary told them her good news. The girls seemed pleased but Joshua said, "Do you think we could have a boy this time?"

It was December before any correspondence came from Dan and

it was only short and to the point with no return address. He didn't mention staying with Adele only that he had waited a month to catch up with Captain Hudson who was still in charge of the ship that had brought him to Australia. Nor did he mention his journey to England, only that he was an officer cadet with a uniform. He had to pass exams that were difficult. He had completed two trips to America but was at present at training college in Dartmouth. He finished by saying he hoped Joshua was still practising his knots so one day he could become a sailor. It was just signed Dan, no special words for Hannah but at least he had finally written.

Joshua was overjoyed at being mentioned, telling all who would listen that he was going to be a sailor just like Dan as soon as he was old enough.

Hannah thought she could probably reply, sending a letter to the college and it would be up to the principal whether it was passed on to Dan. Yes, she decided, that is what she would do so he would know she was thinking of him.

CHAPTER TEN
THE LOSS OF A FAMILY

The dry weather continued with the Governor of the state declaring that water was to be rationed. The vegetables in the garden had withered to nothing and the market stalls had little to sell. They were all patiently waiting for a ship to bring fresh water from the east so Hannah sorted through items that would hold liquid for her to use to fill up at the tap in the yard.

The first people to become sick thought it was due to dehydration but it spread quickly. Joshua was at home with stomach cramps that were made worse by his continual thirst. Several other children became ill and the school was closed as a precaution. Hannah took Amy-Rose, Kitty and Victoria to the shop with her each day so Lizzie could concentrate on Joshua who was by now delirious. The poor lad didn't even have the energy to cry. Lizzie had sent for the doctor but he could only advise them to boil all water and make sure they washed their hands thoroughly.

Hannah had heard that several people had already died, becoming concerned when Lizzie began showing symptoms. Her demise came about quite quickly as she became dehydrated and dizzy. As her blood pressure dropped, the doctor was again called but he only shook his head, saying her body had gone into shock and there was nothing he could do.

Mary offered to come and care for them but Hannah said categorically no. Wasn't she pregnant? It was too much of a risk. In the end Mary and Dennis took the girls to their small flat where they would stay until things improved. Hannah decided to close the shop and stay at home to care for the fading Lizzie and Joshua.

The heat in the house was unbearable even with the windows and door open but there was no breeze. No wind stirred the trees that were so parched that they looked dead. The bark had peeled away, slowly killing them, and everything in this God forsaken land begged for water. The silent crescendo of the forest gave the whole place an eerie feel.

The smell in the house made Hannah want to gag as she emptied the chamber pot. She put a rag over her mouth and nose that had been rubbed with dry herbs when she was attending the sick, not only for the smell but the hope that she wouldn't come down with the illness. The cooker had to be lit to boil water but Hannah soon realised it was better to do this in the evening when it was marginally cooler. Adam would sit with his family when he finished work giving her chance to get some sleep but it seemed futile.

As the days went on neither patient showed any sign of improvement. Those who lived hand to mouth in the shacks were dropping like flies. Bodies were piled onto undertakers carts to be given a collective church service and mass burial.

Hannah was sitting on the veranda when Daniel came up with water and fresh bedding.

Adam asked if he would help to carry the mattress down the narrow stairs and into the sitting room to make Hannah's life a bit easier. The two men removed the few items of furniture out and into the other room, leaving only a comfy chair for Hannah or Adam to rest when they could. Lizzie was half carried, half dragged down the stairs while Hannah stripped the bed to put the sheets on the line to air. There was no possibility of washing anything. She also found a clean nightdress for Lizzie though it would soon be wet through as the fever continued. Adam settled his wife on the makeshift bed while Daniel carried Joshua, who was promptly sick on his shirt. Adam found him a clean one that was too small but covered enough of his torso to get him home.

Hannah stood on the veranda, exhausted, as she said thank you and goodbye to Daniel.

"Please take care of yourself, Hannah," he said. "If anything should happen to you!"

"I've gone through worse. Be on your way and take care yourself." She smiled wearily, putting her hand up in a single wave before going back inside the house.

Filling two mugs with water for her and Adam, she walked back into the room. "The water has boiled but please use the mugs at the back of the draining board if they need a drink. I'm going to try and get some sleep but wake me, you know!"

Adam nodded so she left the room scrubbing her hands until they felt raw before retiring to her bed. It seemed no time at all before Adam tapped on the door, opening it slowly. Looking at the shadows, Hannah realised she had slept for a good few hours and assumed Adam was leaving for work.

"What is it?" she asked when she saw the look on his face.

"He's gone, Joshua's gone," was all he said as he left her to get dressed.

The poor mite had at least died in his sleep. She cleaned the child as best she could, laying him out in a clean shirt, his skin damp and pale. Hannah and Adam used one of the single sheets to wrap his tiny body.

"I'll call in at the undertakers on my way to work and let them know. Will you be alright until then?" Adam asked, feeling hopeless.

This time it was Hannah who just nodded. How was she going to tell Lizzie and Mary or even the girls about this. The cart turned up later that morning to collect Joshua and his small body was placed in the back with the others. It seemed wrong to Hannah to let him go off with strangers but what could she do? Her priority now was to care for Lizzie. They were back two days later to collect Lizzie's body though she hadn't gone so peacefully. She had fought Hannah, screaming and thrashing about, knocking water all over the bed as she fought death. Hannah saw the look of sheer terror in her eyes when she took her last breath. Placing her hands over her eyes to close them, Hannah prayed that she would never have to watch that again. It brought back the misery of losing Mickey when he knew death was upon him. The last thing she could now do for her friend was to make sure she would go to her maker in clean clothes. Hannah brushed the damp hair from Lizzie's brow before praying for her soul.

Even in death Hannah didn't want to leave her friend on her own but she couldn't wait for Adam to return home or it would be too late to get the undertaker's cart. Hannah walked to the family who lived in the shack next to them. They hadn't spoken much apart from once or twice to pass the time of day, so Hannah wasn't sure what her reception would be. As she reached the shack, she wrinkled her nose with the smell. It wasn't just the illness upon them, everything seemed to exude a rancid odour. She offered three pennies to the woman who snatched it as Hannah asked if one of the children could go into town to the undertaker and Adam at work.

The woman screamed at a boy who seemed no more than eight and he set off at a pace into town on his skinny legs and bare feet. Hannah thanked the woman but quickly returned to the house, gulping air as she did. How could anyone live in such terrible conditions? Even with death in her house, it didn't smell as bad as that.

Adam arrived home just as Lizzie was being put in the cart. He looked grey, old, as his shoulders stooped. Putting her hand out to him, Hannah asked, "Do you want to see her before they take her? Perhaps they could be buried together. We could arrange for a plot."

Adam shook his head in despair but it was the undertaker who replied, explaining that it wouldn't be possible as the doctor had declared the illness was dysentery and they would all have to be buried in a mass grave out of town. He continued that the doctor had also told him that it was the water supply and poor hygiene with no sanitation that had caused the problem.

Returning to the house, Adam and Hannah sat at opposite ends of the table. Neither spoke, not knowing what to say to each other. In the end Hannah could stand the silence no longer so went into the room where Lizzie and Joshua had lain, and picking up the bedding she bundled it into a pile. It would have to be burnt as soon as possible, but not tonight, she couldn't face it so she threw it out onto the veranda.

Putting her hands on Adam's shoulders, she said nothing but he did, "Did you know she was going to have another baby?" His voice wavered.

"No, oh no, she never said. I'm so sorry, Adam, truly I am. You've lost three," was all she could say without crying.

Adam stood walking out into the end of the garden where he stood looking into the distance for some time. She left him to his thoughts while she boiled yet more water so she could scrub out the room with hot water and carbolic soap. Hannah was weary to her very soul but didn't want to leave it until tomorrow when she would not have the stomach to tackle it. She needed to keep busy cleaning, cleaning and more cleaning until she was exhausted.

It was getting dark when Adam returned to the house and Hannah felt the need to speak. "I'll go and tell the others tomorrow. Do you need anything Adam? I could warm up some soup but there is nothing else."

"No, I couldn't eat. I think I will just go to bed. I'll take the mattress from Dan's bed, the others will have to be destroyed."

"Yes, yes, good idea. Goodnight." Why had she said that! Of course it wouldn't be a good night tonight or any other night. What was she thinking? A few minutes after Adam went to bed, Hannah climbed up the stairs to her room. This time her prayers were not only for Dan's safety but for the souls of Joshua, Lizzie and the unborn baby who would never have a chance of life. She couldn't understand God's ways at times but would continue with her prayers as promised.

When she woke the following morning Hannah was surprised how late it was. She hadn't heard Adam leave for work and although she had slept deeply, she was weary. Needing to get away from the oppression of the house and the desperate need to talk to someone, she got herself ready for the long walk into town to see Mary. The shimmering heat played tricks on her mind as she walked slowly. It was as though ghostly apparitions appeared and left with the blink of an eye. The defiant sun scorched everything as though bleaching the bright vibrant colours to faded browns and creams. There was no summer pallet because no one knew when summer was any more.

She picked up her pace reaching the shadows of the shops, desperate to hug her children tightly to her, relieved that they were safe for now. Hannah could hear the noise from Mary and the children as she walked up the steps to the small flat. The door was opened by Amy-Rose who immediately rushed to Hannah's outstretched arms. Kitty followed and Mary was about to speak but Hannah shook her head as the tears began to trickle down her cheeks.

"Amy-Rose, take Kitty into the yard to have a game of hopscotch while I have a word with your mam. Go on now," Mary said as she shepherded them out of the room. Amy-Rose was about to protest but saw the look on Mary's face and thought better of it.

Hannah explained briefly what had happened, relaying the conversation with the undertaker and the worry about the children. Mary made a cup of tea, passing a scone to Hannah who realised how hungry she was. She couldn't remember the last time she had eaten but waited while Mary called to the girls to tell them the news. Amy-Rose cried and Kitty followed but Victoria fortunately was too young to really understand, which Hannah was thankful for.

Mary insisted Hannah stay for the day and have dinner with them, telling her Dennis would take her home later. They tried to chat but with their thoughts on their friends, the lulls in the conversation were strained. There was a slight breeze coming off the sea that made the flat feel light and airy when the windows and door was open, though the flat itself was just two rooms above one of the timber shops. It always had the smell of freshly sawn timber that wasn't unpleasant but always left a layer of dust on the floors. The living room come kitchen looked out over the yard with the only door leading to the outside steps. The bedroom looked out onto a narrow passage behind the buildings that went onto the high street. There was no view from either window but Mary had made the place homely.

The children were to stay for a few more days, until after the church service on Sunday, to give Hannah chance to scrub out the house. Dennis would entertain them for an hour while the women were at church. Hannah was invited to come back for lunch before Dennis took them home. The invite was for Adam also but they understood that he may feel the need to be in his own company.

When Hannah told Adam about the service for those who had lost their lives, he refused to go, saying it would not bring them back.

"No it won't but it might bring you some comfort, Adam. Why don't you think about it?" Hannah asked.

"There's nothing to think about. I just want to be left on my own, so would you thank Mary and Dennis but I'll stay here," he replied.

Hannah met Mary at the church gate and they walked down the path with the many others for the burial service. They linked arms to support each other. Instead of individual funerals that many couldn't afford, the names of the deceased were read out with the date of death. Joshua Quinn 10/12/1878 before Elizabeth Quinn 12/12/1878 but there was no mention of her unborn child. It was terribly sad to hear the families who had lost so many and of all ages.

The Reverend said, "Life is here and gone with the blink of an eye. Like the wind that passes in a moment, but in that short time they are with us we should give thanks and rejoice to the Almighty in the hope of resurrection to eternal life through our Lord Jesus Christ, Amen."

The congregation repeated, "Amen", their heads bowed in their thoughts for their loved ones. A Book of Remembrance had been placed in the apse with all the names but Hannah assumed many would not be able to read it so it was scant comfort.

The children were happy to be back in their own home. Hannah was sure Mary was relieved to have the place back to herself again. She decided she would open the shop as she hadn't received any income for a few weeks and she didn't want to use any more of her savings. The school hadn't yet re-opened and the girls groaned at the thought of spending the day in the shop but they took their rag dolls with them. Amy-Rose was much quieter than her usual argumentative self but Hannah decided to leave it, as she didn't have the energy to argue with her eldest daughter.

There didn't seem to be any point in having any great celebrations for Christmas nor the New Year of 1879 as so many were still in mourning. The epidemic seemed to have abated now that water could be collected from hand pumps in the town. Hannah continued to fill containers from the tap in the yard of the shop and pull it home on the bogey. Filling up the containers was a task she had given to the unwilling Amy-Rose when she returned from school that had re-opened in the New Year.

Mary came to the shop each day to collect Victoria and it was nice to see her pregnancy progressing well. Hannah was relieved to have a little time on her own because she still had to do all the washing, cooking, cleaning and caring when she got home.

Adam had retreated to a place where even Victoria couldn't reach and Hannah worried about him but didn't know how to talk to him as she seemed so busy with one thing and another. She decided he was better to get over his loss in his own way just as she had with Mickey. He still chopped wood but there was nothing in the garden for him to attend to and he spent most of his evenings sitting on the veranda steps looking out into space. Hannah knew she would have to talk to him about their future but was afraid to broach the subject. Instead they continued in the same manner with the two of them just muddling along in the heat.

CHAPTER ELEVEN

IS THE WORST OVER?

The temperature had been inferno hot for weeks and everyone was wrung out with sweat. It only cooled slightly in the evening, making it almost impossible to sleep. One day led to another where tempers frayed, food was expensive even if there was anything to buy. Hannah heard there had been riots so the state governor had asked Britain for help with provisions but the ships were weeks away.

In the distance there was a rumbling of thunder with dry cracks of lightning. The air was still, waiting for something to happen. There was a clap of thunder. Hannah counted to the lightning. It was getting closer. The sky darkened to a deep dark black which made the lightning even more spectacular. She stood in the doorway, looking over the veranda to the distant hills. They looked as though they were dancing to a light show but the light didn't disappear when the lightning ceased.

The earth was parched. Brittle trees became crisp as fires burned in the distance. Hannah had never seen anything like it as the fires grew bigger, smoke billowing into the dark sky. She watched in horror as the lightning bolts struck the ground, getting closer and closer. She was afraid they would reach the edge of the settlement but there was nothing she could do but watch. As if by divine intervention, big heavy drops of rain began to fall, slowly at first, like freckles, the dull thwack as they hit the ground, red earth puffing up into a cloud of dust. Just one or two before the heavens opened into a deluge. She breathed in the smell of the dry earth as it tried to soak up the water in its thirst. Everything was desperate for water, the stream had dried up months ago, and the garden had nothing to grow.

Hannah rushed outside to let the rain flow over her head, soaking her in a moment. She laughed out loud as she put her face to the sky, drinking in the rain. Within minutes she was drenched through, her hair falling about her as she danced somewhat manically, not caring if anyone was watching her.

She thought of where she would always call home, winters of unrelenting sleet and blizzards. It reminded her of Northend and Annie, her friends, the small school. In England they had defined seasons and they never went too long without rain. This last year had been one of unrelenting heat and for the first time in a long time she felt homesick and it saddened her.

The children were afraid of the loud noise as the rain hammered on the roof. They were gathered in Hannah's bed as the downpour continued long into the night. There was an orchestra of rain, drums beating down onto the roof, while the percussion had a more delicate tune as it plopped into pots strewn around the top floor. It was somehow calming to Hannah and although the bed was full of arms and legs, she did eventually manage to get some sleep.

The sun rose the following morning to smoke still spiralling from the burnt out fires, giving the sky streaks of red and orange interspersed with grey clouds as the rain continued. It lasted for days until the earth couldn't take any more and the place became a quagmire. No one complained, they just hoped the worst was over.

The sky returned to an azure blue while white clouds scudded across the sky and Hannah realised for the first time in almost a year she could hear the buzzing of insects among the new grass and leaves. Not only that, but the pretty birds had returned, giving the trees a rainbow effect with their bright colours. The wildlife was making up for lost time and she was full of wonder at how quickly this happened. Suddenly seedlings were sprouting all over the garden as busy bees pollinated any flowers they could find.

The stream at the bottom of the garden was now running freely but Hannah worried about using the water, still preferring to take the bogey into town to fill containers from the stand pipe, though when it was heavy it stuck in the mud.

The rain continued on and off for weeks but thankfully they had no more thunder and lightning. Hannah rejoiced that the water had only reached the bottom of the veranda steps. The families in the shacks had been flooded out as the water ran freely through the cramped space. Clothing and bedding was now strewn onto makeshift clothes lines after being saturated and they were more filthy than before, if that were possible. Even in the rain, the children ran feral as they playing along the road and in and out of the shacks in bigger and bigger gangs. Amy-Rose wanted to play with them which Hannah forbade. She didn't think she was better than anyone else, she really didn't, but she wouldn't allow her daughter to run with them and was pleased when school re-opened after the holidays.

Life returned to a routine for Hannah as the shop became busier with a quick turnover of goods. People were arriving on ships all the time. Even Dennis was extremely busy providing timber for the houses now being built on the other side of town. They looked palatial compared to the shacks and even their small house. They had wooden painted clapboard and large windows which looked out to sea, picket fences finished off the grand feel.

The genteel ladies brought English fashion into the growing town. Hannah often watched from the shop doorway, Victoria on her hip, while she waited for the girls to finish school. The ladies' dresses were in muted colours of pale blue, lilacs, creams and pinks which was in contrast to the loud colours of the hotel women or the greys and browns of the rest. They strolled among the shops wearing satin shoes, lace gloves, carrying matching parasols to hide their pale faces from the sun.

Hannah's girls were doing well at school but she missed having something to read herself, if she got time having to make do with her bible that she must have read hundreds of times. Mary still called in most days that always cheered her up. Her pregnancy was going well. Dennis had made a wooden perambulator that he painted white, and the farrier had made a frame with a handle so Mary would be able to push it. However Mary was quite superstitious and wouldn't have it in the flat before the baby's birth so it sat in the shop taking up valuable space. It did give Hannah a chance, when the shop was quiet, to make bedding as a surprise gift for her friend.

In the early hours of 16 May 1879 Mary gave birth to a daughter who weighed just over five pounds. Her hair was a deep red, eyes a haunting emerald green. She was a most beautiful baby. Mary was somewhat overwhelmed that she had managed to produce such a perfect child. Dennis called her his Irish Colleen but there was only one name suitable so she became Ruby O'Reilly. Hannah was delighted for her friends who were besotted with their daughter. It was wonderful to have a new life after the terrible tragedy of the last year.

Hannah hadn't heard from Dan for more than a year even though she checked regularly with Mrs Coyle, the postmistress. Locking the shop door one afternoon, holding Victoria's hand, she walked along the shaded path into the hardware shop that doubled as a post office and haberdashery to check for any post. Two ladies were looking at ribbons while Hannah stood waiting for a gentleman to collect a parcel. Mrs Coyle shook her head toward Hannah who was about to leave when she heard one of the women say, "That's her! Living with a man whose wife died last year. She's even bringing up his child as her own. It's a disgrace."

Hannah felt she had to defend herself so she walked closer to the women. "For your information, ladies, I am a widow who owns half the house I am living in. The gentleman who lives there owns the other half. Indeed I look after his daughter while he goes to his place of work. What would you have me do? Abandon them? We have all had to pull together in this God forsaken place. Perhaps one of you would be good enough to provide me with rent free accommodation in one of your homes? I'm sure you would have space? We would be no trouble, my children are house trained. Well, what do you say?" She stared at them both before closing the door loudly, leaving everyone in the shop stunned at her outburst.

Hannah was smarting. How dare they talk about her like that? She mulled over the conversation, worrying that people perceived her and Adam as living together. Well, yes, they were living in the same house and he gave her money to buy food for him and Victoria. He would just tip the money onto the table each week. They hadn't discussed whether it was enough. He still did the chopping of the wood and what he could in the garden and anything heavy while she did the washing, cooking, cleaning, so she supposed in a way they were living like a couple. It upset her that people were talking about her but she wasn't sure what she could do about it. If she moved into the rooms above the shop while Daniel was away, she would still get talked about and where would he go when he was home. In the end she gave herself a headache thinking about it so decided she needed to have a conversation with Mary and Dennis before she approached Adam with the problem.

She knew she wouldn't be able to rent somewhere without selling her half of the house even though she still had savings from the sale of the land. The other problem would be what to do with Victoria who was now approaching school age. Hannah thought she could have her before and after school so Adam could go to work but it would be no life for a small child living in that house with a father who seemed to have forgotten Victoria was his. She looked half heartedly at what was available to rent closer to town but nothing seemed suitable, too small, too expensive or in the wrong place. In the end Hannah gave up, vowing to make the best of things for now.

Since Lizzie's demise, Adam had begun drinking sometimes after work. At first it was one or two each Friday when he got paid. Hannah didn't like it but felt it wasn't her place to say anything about it. The smell still made her want to retch so she made sure she was in her bed before he got home if possible. He had taken to sleeping in the downstairs sitting room so Hannah felt relatively safe upstairs but kept the girls in the room with her. She wasn't sure how much longer she could put up with it. She would love to sell her half of the house and move nearer town but who would want a half of a house? She had been thinking about it for some time as she had never liked the long walk but she had to make a plan before she approached Adam.

CHAPTER TWELVE

MAKING A LIFE

As the year of 1882 began, Hannah looked at her family, amazed at how much they had grown and how time had passed so quickly. She couldn't even say after all this time that she was totally happy in Australia, she wasn't, but she would never have enough money for them all to travel back to England and start again. She couldn't leave her best friend Mary behind either so she had to be content with what she had.

Amy-Rose was approaching twelve and determined to leave school. Hannah was having the very same conversation that she had had with Dan. Her daughter wasn't vacuous exactly, she was good at her schoolwork but all she wanted to do was have nice clothes and marry a rich man so she wouldn't have to work.

Although Hannah was biased, Amy-Rose was a beautiful child. When she was born, she was like her father with his dark hair but this had lightened to a strawberry blonde that was enhanced by her pale skin and rosebud lips. Even at her young age she was a bonny girl, though she was always preening herself, throwing her hair back provocatively, Hannah thought.

She also had a temper on her and they argued about what would happen if she left school. Hannah wanted her to stay until she was fourteen to get her school certificate though she could legally leave at twelve. She was frustrated at what she saw as her daughter's impudence and this led to an impasse with tension in the house. In the end Hannah lay the law down, saying that if she did leave school she would have to pay for her keep by doing all the cooking, cleaning and washing while Hannah worked at the shop. No she wouldn't, came back the reply. She wouldn't be incarcerated in that house all day every day. Instead she would find a job to earn her own money.

Hannah talked to Mary many times on the subject but asked her not to interfere, feeling it would undermine her authority if she did so. In the end Hannah told Amy-Rose she could leave school if she could find suitable employment, knowing it would be almost impossible.

Amy-Rose left the shop one Saturday morning in her best dress and bonnet sure she would return with a job of some description. After a few hours Hannah was becoming concerned and was about to shut up the shop to look for her when the girl flounced in, throwing the door wide open. She didn't speak but walked into the back room and drank a mug of water before flopping into a chair. Hannah watched her daughter remove her bonnet but remained quiet as the look on Amy-Rose's face was like thunder.

She left her to contemplate and it was after the meal that evening before she spoke about her experience. She had tried everywhere. The women were nasty to her but the men just stared at her, she stated. Mrs Coyle at the hardware store made it clear they wouldn't take her on as her sort came from the wrong side of the track.

"Never mind, at least you tried," Hannah said as gently as possible. "I have an idea."

Amy-Rose pulled a face but Hannah stopped her from speaking. "If you stay at school I will teach you about the shop. You can work there on a Saturday and I will pay you a wage."

"How much will you pay me?" Amy-Rose asked eagerly.

"Well I thought threepence until you are trained to go out to the auctions and then we can look at it again." Hannah looked at her daughter.

"That won't buy me anything. I need new clothes. Look at my dress, it's faded everywhere." Amy-Rose almost spat the words out. "No, I'll go to the hotel and ask about work, after all it was good enough for auntie Mary."

"My God, you won't, girl. You'll be eaten alive. Now let's say no more about it and finish your meal." Hannah was distraught at her daughter's insolence. She would have to speak to Mary to see if she would drop a word to the proprietor on the quiet to stop her taking the girl on. The men would want to take her, she was sure of that even though she was still a child, and it would be over her dead body that it would happen. In the end it worked out better than expected from Hannah's point of view.

Mary gave Hannah the nod that she had spoken to Mrs Jobson at the hotel and she was prepared to speak to Amy-Rose. Hannah told her she could call in the following Saturday morning but to be prepared for menial work as she had no experience.

In a way Hannah felt sorry for the girl when she returned in less than an hour and burst into tears. She explained the only vacancy was mainly cleaning out the cellar. She couldn't even move the barrels of ale. She would have to scrub floors as well as the stairwell on her hands and knees before washing the smelly tankards. Her hands would be sore and her hair would smell of beer, she continued. Hannah tried not to laugh at her daughter's obvious distress.

"What did you think you would be doing?" Hannah asked. "Poor Mary had sore hands and an aching back working the laundry but she never complained."

"Well, I'm not going to do it. I'm going to ask uncle Adam if he can get me a job in the courts. There must be something I can do. My English is good and so is my maths," Amy-Rose stated before stomping out of the room.

Amy-Rose wasted no time in asking Adam the very question and he was serious in his response, as though he was interviewing her, asking what her qualifications were and what experience she had.

"You know I can read and write better than the teachers and I am very good at mathematics," Amy-Rose replied expectantly.

"Do you have your school certificate?"

"No, you know I don't."

"I'm sorry, Miss Phelan, but you would need a minimum of your school certificate. Ask me again when you have that," Adam said kindly.

Hannah watched as Amy-Rose pushed past everyone and up the stairs to the bedroom, not wanting to speak to anyone. She knew she would think it wasn't fair. Most of the children in her class would be leaving school at twelve, the boys to become labourers whilst the girls would help out at home or find menial jobs in other houses. Hannah knew Amy-Rose thought she was better than that and in the main that was her fault for keeping her away from other children. After she had calmed down, Amy-Rose returned to the kitchen, telling her mother that she would remain at school until she had her certificate.

Hannah was relieved, telling her she had made the right decision. It surprised her that there were no more tantrums and she took to helping the younger children with their letters. The teacher offered to give her a good reference to go with her school certificate and that seemed to placate her.

They continued the long walk into town each day but Hannah never felt any better about it. They still had to go past the shacks though many of them were now uninhabited, falling down, making the place look a mess. The poverty of those left behind was there for all to see. She was still unsettled in the house and now she had sorted the problem with Amy-Rose she knew she would have to talk to Adam about selling up but it never seemed the right time.

However it was Adam who broached the subject first when he arrived home one evening with a leaflet he had been given. The Governor was borrowing money from Britain, was using it to put water and sewerage into their part of the town so better housing could be provided. The leaflet said the state would purchase the land or re-home people when new properties were built to rent on the other side of the river. He knew she didn't like walking into town but the biggest problem would be finding somewhere suitable.

In the end they agreed Adam should find out more about the scheme and what money they would receive before any decisions were made. Hannah was of the opinion that any money she received would be better than the situation she was in at the moment and she still had savings from the land sale but it wouldn't last forever.

Adam didn't wait to find out what was going on before shocking her further by telling her he was going off to look for gold. The men he drank with said they could make their fortunes by travelling to the interior at Broken Hill. It could set him up for life, he told her, with an excitement in his voice she hadn't heard before. There were a number of men who had been before and were due to travel together in the next few weeks. The men were known as 'cameleers' who had trekked through deserts in Egypt although they were known locally as 'Afghans'.

Hannah had seen them camping on waste ground, lighting fires in the evening. Their camels were hobbled to stop them wandering off at night. They would be loaded with provisions to last the journey and to barter with at the outstations.

Hannah was amazed at how much Adam knew. She had always been afraid of the dark skinned men not to mention the strange animals. As far as she was concerned, they were peculiar looking, smelly animals, but then all animals were strange in Australia.

"What about Victoria?" she asked.

"She could stay with you, couldn't she? I thought I could write an affidavit making her your ward. The money from the sale of my share of the house should be more than enough to keep her until I get back!" Adam said, the latter more of an afterthought.

"It seems you have it all planned without the decency of mentioning to me," Hannah said crossly.

"Well you are hardly my wife and I have made my decision but if you don't want her I am sure Mary would be only too happy to take her on," he said, his voice becoming louder.

"Don't want her? Oh Adam, you make her sound like a commodity. I love that child as though she was my own. Of course I will care for her but she needs her father."

"No, she doesn't. She needs a mother but she's not here, is she?" he said accusingly.

"That's not my fault, you know that. I did my best for Lizzie and

Joshua so don't shout at me, Adam. I miss them as well but if you are determined to go then I'll manage as I always have."

"I could sell my share of the house and you could remain here if you wanted to. I'm sure your good friend Samuel Fletcher would be happy to share a house with you. He told me he wanted to walk out with you, asking what were his chances. It would solve all your problems if you married him."

"Shut up, shut up. There is no way I would walk out, as you say, with that man. Don't, just don't sell your share of the house to him, Adam, I warn you." Hannah was almost in tears.

"You warn me? What will you do? Kill me like your first husband? I think I should be warning you, Hannah. I could go to the polis and tell them what Samuel Fletcher told me. I'm not even going to ask you if it's true. I can see it by the look on your face." He banged his fist on the table making her jump.

"No, it's not. It's lies, all lies. That man has made it up and it's shocked me to think he is spreading these lies to anyone who will listen. I don't know why he would want to do me harm, I really don't, only that I have rejected his advances. Please Adam, I'm begging you to believe me." Hannah cried but she knew he didn't.

Running out onto the veranda, Hannah was frightened, more frightened than she had been in a long time. Who else had that man talked to, who else knew her secret? She thought she had managed to put it to the back of her mind and front it out. Now Adam was using it to threaten her and there wasn't a thing she could do about it. He would think what he wanted and whatever she said now he wouldn't believe her. The only person she could talk to was Daniel. He always knew what to do.

Returning to the kitchen, she walked past Adam, not looking at him, but said, "Just make sure the paperwork is in order before you leave," before climbing the stairs to bed.

Hannah told Mary what Adam was planning to do, not about Samuel Fletcher, no that was for Daniel only. Within a week Adam had left his job, packed a bag and was ready to set off on his journey. Everyone was in town to watch the expedition set off, wives hugging husbands while children were waving as though it was a carnival. There was even a band of sorts playing as the rabble of men set off behind the 'cameleers', down the main street past the market stalls where banners had been put up like a celebration parade.

For Hannah, her life was to change once again. She was now a widow with three children and would soon be homeless once the sale of the house to the government went through. She had struggled to find anywhere suitable close to town and for what she could afford knew it would be almost impossible. She thought if she was stuck she could ask Daniel if they could move into the rooms above the shop until something came up. She didn't feel safe in the house with Adam gone. She felt vulnerable and kept a piece of wood under the bed to protect her family if need be. The house had never felt like a home since the death of Mickey. They'd had such high hopes of making a good life when they first bought it but now it was like a millstone around her neck.

It was while she was in the shop that she came up with an idea to put a notice in the window asking for rooms to rent, writing it in her best handwriting, hoping she wouldn't get too many cranks. Mary and Dennis had offered to move in with her and rent Adam's share of the house but Hannah just wanted to put it all behind her and start again.

Over a week went by and Hannah had no luck with the notice in the window. It was while she was filling water containers in the yard that a woman she knew as Mrs Wilkie came out from the property next door. Their paths didn't cross very often. Hannah hadn't realised that her husband had died, leaving the woman alone. It was as Hannah was passing on her condolences that Mrs Wilkie told her she was looking to rent out a room to make an income. Hannah asked to have a look though thought it would be far too small for her and three children.

The house had the same layout as the shop but Hannah saw immediately that the rooms were much bigger. The kitchen was square, making it big enough to take her large table and chairs. Mrs Wilkie had a small sofa in the kitchen where she spent most of her time. The front parlour was another square room with a door and large window looking out onto the main street. Upstairs were two bedrooms, one much larger than the other. Hannah thought the larger room would take the two sets of bunk beds though they would not have much space and no room for anything else.

Mrs Wilkie offered to move into the smaller bedroom and a weekly rent was agreed until Hannah could find somewhere bigger. Hannah agreed to provide all the housekeeping as she was feeding more people and for them both it seemed sensible. She was happy with the deal and happy that she would not have to have that long walk everyday, and the girls would be able to go to school on their own. Although she didn't say it she was also pleased that she would be closer to Daniel.

It wasn't long before Hannah had packed up all her belongings and stood waiting for Dennis and Daniel to arrive with the cart. The girls were with Mary and as she shut the door she was relieved rather than sad that she was finally leaving her marital home.

Sitting between the two men, she didn't look back as the horse set off down the road, for her it would be the last time. The cart had to be unloaded in the main street and Hannah was glad when Daniel re-built the beds. The table and chairs were now in the kitchen and everything else was left in boxes in the parlour to be unpacked later.

The two women found it difficult at first, seeming to get in each other's way and Hannah was afraid the girls would be too boisterous for Mrs Wilkie, Maggie. It took a while for the house to settle into some kind of order but Hannah was certainly much happier away from her old home. She was still awaiting the money from the sale and she wasn't sure what to do with Adam's share as she didn't trust the bank. She thought it would be a good idea to sew it to the bottom of the mattress until she could make a decision.

With all the new housing proposed on the outskirts of town, the owner of the timber yard asked Dennis to employ extra men. He asked Daniel and bought another horse and cart for him to use. He also took on two young boys to train. It meant Daniel was home each evening and Hannah began cooking him an evening meal along with their own. She thought it was the least she could do when he had given her the shop, though she wasn't comfortable asking him to have his meal with them. She didn't know what Maggie would think as she was a little straight laced. As he arrived home after they had eaten she would just plate his up and send Amy-Rose or Kitty through with it.

Over the months Hannah and Daniel became closer, she would often pop in to see him once the children were in bed. They were happy in each others' company, both knowing what they couldn't say. When he announced it was his birthday, Hannah was disappointed that she hadn't known and therefore not bought him a present. He asked for a hug which she gave him willingly. They both liked the closeness of each other, something they both missed. Daniel leant in to kiss her gently. He wanted much more, but didn't want to spoil the moment. In the end he took her hand in his, saying, "We'll be alright, won't we?"

Hannah confirmed that they would.

CHAPTER THIRTEEN

ONE THING LEADS TO ANOTHER

With the blink of an eye it was May 1883 and Amy-Rose was almost ready to leave school. Hannah didn't know what to do with her. She didn't think there would be enough to do in the shop, like today. It was a slow morning and Hannah was becoming bored. She had dusted all the tables, moved items into more prominent positions and was in the kitchen washing glassware when she heard the bell. Drying her hands quickly, she walked back into the shop to see a smartly dressed gentleman who removed his hat to show a head of dark curly hair fastened loosely at the nape of his neck with a ribbon.

He smiled as he spoke. "You must be the sister of Amy-Rose Phelan," he said, holding out his hand. "My name is Gabriel Brown."

Taking his hand Hannah returned his smile, "Flattery will get you nowhere, sir. I am the girl's mother. How can I help you? She's not in any trouble, is she?" Hannah said the latter as an afterthought.

"No, no trouble at all," he responded. "On the contrary, your daughter very kindly returned my wallet which I had dropped on the pavement last time I was in town. She refused a reward and we chatted for a short while."

"Amy-Rose didn't mention any of this to me, sir. As I said, how may I help you?" Hannah was more than puzzled as it was unlike her daughter not to mention, never mind bore everyone to death with talking about it and that was a mystery in itself.

"Miss Phelan explained she was finishing school shortly and would be looking for employment once she had her school certificate," Mr Brown continued. "She is a credit to you, madam, a well spoken bright young lady."

"Thank you, sir. She has her moments. As for work, I have told her she can help me in the shop but she thinks it is below her, being what she calls shop work." Hannah smiled. "But I am at a loss as to why you are here."

"That's the crux of the matter, Mrs Phelan, may I call you that?" Hannah nodded and he continued, "My wife has been ill since the birth of our fourth child. To be truthful, she has taken to her bed. I think she feels out of place here in Australia. The servants and the nursemaids look after the day to day running of the house and children. I'm out all day and I think she misses conversation with someone."

"You've lost me, Mr Brown. What has this got to do with Amy-Rose?" Hannah was even more puzzled.

"After chatting to your daughter, I wondered if she would consider a role of lady's maid and companion to my wife when she finishes school."

"Oh, well, sir, you have put me on the spot somewhat. As I said, this is all news to me. You seem to have had a long conversation with my daughter and now are offering her a position in your household. With all due respect, I know nothing about you or your family."

"Well as I said, my name is Gabriel Brown and I am the chief engineer here to facilitate the enlargement of the port. I can assure you that my intentions toward your daughter are genuine. There doesn't seem to be too many well-educated young ladies in the colony. I assume your daughter has you to thank for that?" Mr Brown nodded toward Hannah.

She couldn't take it all in. "I'm not sure that would be a good idea. Amy-Rose is just a child. She is not used to caring for someone else. There are too many things to think about."

"I appreciate what you are saying, Mrs Phelan, but let's not be too hasty. The girl needs a job and I have a vacancy. What say you to coming to the house on Sunday for a spot of tea where we can discuss the matter further. Your daughter can talk to my wife and we will see how that goes?" he said. "I can send a trap for you about four. Would that be suitable?"

"I'm sorry, that would be difficult," Hannah replied. "I have two other daughters, Kitty and Victoria, I would have to make arrangements for them." She wondered why she had said that as Mary or Maggie would have had them for a few hours.

"Well bring them along. My elder ones can entertain them, I am sure." He laughed.

"Alright but I will need to talk it over with my friend, Mr Jerrold, he is a sort of father figure since my husband passed over."

"Bring him along, might as well make an outing." His laugh was infectious and Hannah joined in, shaking his hand.

As he opened the door, he gave Hannah a salute. "Until Sunday."

The glassware remained in the sink while Hannah mulled over the conversation. She was surprised, very surprised, that Amy-Rose hadn't given them chapter and verse several times.

The shop bell brought her back to the present as three men walked into the shop. One of them was Samuel Fletcher who she hadn't seen for some time but now here he was large as life with men she assumed were his friends.

"How can I help you, gentlemen?" Hannah's voice was shaking but she looked toward the two men who stood staring intently at her.

"Mrs Phelan, looking as lovely as ever," Samuel Fletcher said. "I thought I would call and reacquaint ourselves. I have a proposition to put to you. I'm looking for a wife and you have no husband. These gentlemen are here to confirm the terms of the agreement. Don't look so shocked, you and I have known each other for a lot of years and it is only a matter of time before you agree."

Hannah couldn't speak. She had hoped that she would never see this man again. From what Adam had told her, she was sure Samuel Fletcher knew about her first husband but keeping up the pretence, said, "I am not interested in marrying you or anyone else and I would ask you and your friends to leave."

The men remained where they were but Hannah could say no more.

"I told you she had spirit, didn't I?" Samuel Fletcher said to his friends, "but it will only be a matter of time before you are mine, I will make sure of that." He leered at her.

The doorbell went again and Mary was preceded into the shop by the perambulator that now held two children. Mary had given birth to a second daughter Corrine on 23 October 1881. She didn't have the red hair of her sister though her emerald green eyes were as large and round. Ruby was now four and a madam. She was sitting uncomfortably in the pram creating a din because she had wanted to walk. Mary was blooming as she was pregnant for the third time.

The pram took up most of the shop and the noise made the men make a hasty retreat but not before Samuel Fletcher passed pleasantries with Mary, ending with, "Think about my offer, Mrs Phelan, and I will be back at a more suitable time for your answer."

As always Hannah was pleased to see Mary and never more so than at this moment. Seeing that man again had shaken her, making her feel afraid, very afraid for her family. Picking Ruby out of the pram, she let her down in the kitchen, giving her one of the girls' rag dolls to play with. Corrine lay in the pram, eyes darting everywhere. Putting the lock on the door, Hannah went back into the kitchen and flopped into the chair.

Before her friend could speak, Hannah said, "Oh Mary, I've had the strangest morning. Wait until I tell you who had been into the shop and why."

"Well I can see that man Fletcher was here and he has shaken you. Look at your hands. What has he said to make you so upset? I don't trust that man, I really don't, he's shifty," Mary continued.

"Oh he had the nerve to ask me to marry him with his henchmen in support. You are right, he has shaken me. He frightens me, to tell the truth, but let's not talk about him. It's the other visitor who is much more interesting." Hannah picked up her cup of tea, spilling some on the table but went on. "Do you know a gentleman by the name of Gabriel Brown?"

"Only that Dennis has mentioned he has delivered to his house, the one overlooking Anglesey Point to the sea. Why, what do you want to know about him?" Mary replied.

Hannah told her the tale which was punctuated with, "Well I never," and "I don't believe it", for Amy-Rose not to say anything.

"I wouldn't have minded a look at the place myself. Do you think he'd mind me tagging along," Mary laughed.

"It will be bad enough with us lot there, like a charabanc trip for the poor. I don't know what Daniel will think when I tell him about the invite." Hannah's laugh was somewhat forced.

"Changing the subject," Mary said, "haven't you talked to him about, you know, your situation? Well I know you haven't, otherwise you would have told me."

"What can I say? It's me who who won't live with him, over the brush so to speak."

Mary let out a bellow of a laugh, making Corrine jump, crying out loudly. Picking her up to feed her, Mary said, "I haven't heard that saying for years. Yer getting right common, Mrs Phelan, that you are," as they both had a fit of giggles.

"I can't broach the subject, can I?" Hannah explained. "He said Adele would never give him a divorce and I can't live with him. I really can't."

"No but it's more than seven years since he left and he could ask for an annulment through the court," Mary said with some authority.

"I can't say if you want me to be your wife, Daniel, you need to spend money seeking a divorce, can I?" Hannah replied.

"Well you don't need to put it like that."

They both laughed again.

Hannah thought what a tonic Mary was. She had been upset at the visit of Samuel Fletcher but had put him out of her mind for a few hours. She never saw bad in anyone. Marriage and motherhood was Mary to a 't', she was a natural. How lucky she was to have met her all those years ago. They were still laughing when someone hammered on the shop door.

Hannah was worried about answering it but saw it was the girls home from school. After the hellos and what have you been doing at school, Mary stood, putting Corrine back into the pram. "If I don't have tea on the table, I'll end up with a black eye," she laughed.

"Auntie Mary, is that true? Would uncle Dennis really give you a black eye?" Kitty enquired with a worried look on her face.

"Aye lass, you lot think he's a saint but he's got a temper on him, I can tell you." Mary ruffled Kitty's hair. "No, of course not. He's the kindest man I have ever met. I was lucky when I found him. He makes me the happiest woman alive."

"Give over, we'll all be falling at his feet next time we see him. Saint Dennis, that's got a ring to it." Hannah gave Mary a hug. "We're the lucky ones meeting you, now go on before we end up in tears."

Instead the tears came from Ruby who kicked and screamed at the thought at being put back into the pram. Her body rigid while she held her breath, Hannah thought at least she was quiet but then she started screeching again.

"I'll walk back with you, auntie Mary," Amy-Rose said, taking Ruby by the hand.

"Me too," said Kitty.

"And me." Victoria didn't want to be left out.

"Go on then but come straight back and no talking to strangers." Hannah looked straight at Amy-Rose who gave her mother a puzzled look. She watched them walk along the path, Ruby happily holding Amy-Rose and Kitty's hands while Victoria was helping to push the pram. That was her family, Hannah thought, a proper house of girls.

Quickly rinsing the glasses that were now sitting in cold water, Hannah left them to drain while peeling the vegetables for the evening meal. She would carry the pans next door when the girls returned and she could shut up the shop for the day. Now she was alone her mind went back to the conversation with that man. She couldn't say his name even in her mind. What could she do about his persistence? She would have to talk to Daniel again. He would know what to do.

It was while they were sitting around the table eating their evening meal that Hannah spoke to her eldest daughter. "You seem to have a gentleman friend, Amy-Rose. Did you not think to mention it to me?"

"Why, what did he say?" she replied, looking embarrassed, knowing to whom she was referring.

"It seems you made quite an impression on Mr Gabriel Brown, so tell me what happened?" Hannah asked. When she was satisfied with what Amy-Rose said, she relayed the conversation with Mr Brown and the girls all squealed with delight.

Later in the evening Hannah slipped in to see Daniel who was eating his meal at the small table in the kitchen. He stood when he saw Hannah's shadow pass the window, opening his arms as she stepped inside. There was no embarrassment between them as he kissed her gently. When they parted, Hannah smiled. "I have an invitation for you, Mr Jerrold. Sunday best will be required," she said and went on to tell him about her visitor.

"How did she manage to keep that a secret?" Daniel held out a chair for Hannah. "It could be the making of her. She has always thought she was better than everyone else. But why on earth do I need to go? I'll have to be on my best behaviour, no cussing or blaspheming."

"Amy-Rose will be determined to take the position and I just want someone on my side to look for the pitfalls. Say you'll come." Hannah took his hand.

"I'll always be on your side, Hannah, you know that. But what's wrong? You look as though you are about to burst into tears? I always have that effect on you." Daniel tried to laugh.

"You might not be when I tell you who else came into the shop today." Hannah told him about Samuel Fletcher and his proposal. "I'm afraid he'll go to the polis or harm the girls. I'm frightened, Daniel, really frightened of him. You know he told Adam what he knew about me so who else is he telling, I ask you?"

"What's done is done, Hannah. You can't change the past but it's what you learn from it that counts. Don't let it worry you. I'll sort it. He obviously can't take no for an answer."

"What will you do?" she asked. "I don't want you to get into trouble on my account but I just can't carry on being frightened like this all the time."

"I've been in trouble since the day I met you, Hannah, so it's too late now. Anyway you don't need to know. As I said, just leave it to me. He won't bother you again." Daniel said it with more confidence than he felt.

As she got up, Daniel tried to kiss her but she pulled away. "Aw Hannah, you're testing my will. How much longer will I have to wait?"

"You know the answer to that, Daniel," she replied. "Goodnight."

Their hands slipped apart as she left him looking toward her.

CHAPTER FOURTEEN

HOW THE OTHER HALF LIVES

The trap arrived at exactly four o'clock outside the front of the shop. Daniel was already standing uncomfortably outside, as was Mary, Dennis and the children as Maggie joined them waiting to wave them off as though they were going on a journey. Daniel lightened the mood by bowing to Amy-Rose as he helped her into the trap and she took his hand, picking up her skirt before placing her foot on the step. She looked at her boot, which although polished was shabby and old.

Hannah's stomach had been churning all afternoon with the worry of losing her daughter just as she had lost her son at the same age.

The driver introduced himself as Ned, and Daniel jumped up beside him, looking uncomfortable in his shirt and jacket. The younger girls waved to the small gathering as they headed off toward the markets and the road that meandered up the hill until they forked right. Hannah had never been this way before. Yes, she had been up to Arthur's Point but they turned into what proclaimed was private property. After a few hundred yards the trap stopped so Daniel jumped down to open the gates.

The house had a large white fence all around and a sweeping drive to the front where the carts and carriages could turn. The trap stopped in front of a set of steps leading up to a wide veranda. Hannah didn't know this kind of house existed in Australia. It looked like the old manor houses from home except it was built from wood. She was astounded at the number of people rushing in all directions; butlers, maids, outside workers seemed to be everywhere. It was like a small town on its own.

Gabriel Brown came bounding down the steps to greet them, shepherding Kitty and Victoria toward a woman in a grey dress, white apron and mob cap. She bobbed her knee before taking the girls' hands, moving toward the open door. Kitty looked back for reassurance and Hannah nodded as they disappeared into the large hallway. Mr Brown introduced himself, shaking hands firmly with Daniel, Hannah and lastly with Amy-Rose. He swept his long arms wide, saying, "Come and meet my wife."

Mrs Brown was sitting in a comfy chair, in the shade, next to a large round table with a delicate lace tablecloth over but it groaned with sandwiches, pies, tarts, cakes and glasses with a large pitcher of homemade lemonade.

Hannah almost commented on the fare but remembered her manners. Mr Brown introduced his wife, Isabel, her skin a delicate porcelain white, and she held out her hand as though it was a leaden weight.

They sat at the table while maids fussed around them. Mr Brown was a convivial host, talking generally as they ate and drank. He chatted to Daniel about his work on the new harbour, and he in turn talked about his time on the railroad and how he was now working at the timber yard. Mrs Brown said very little, picking at her food that had been placed on a side table for her.

When their appetite was sated, Mr Brown stood. "Well, as usual the kitchen staff have prepared a feast fit for a king. Miss Phelan, why don't you sit and talk to my wife while I take Mr Jerrold and your mother for a look around the house?"

Hannah gave Amy-Rose a look that said a million things to reassure the girl.

The house was as resplendent inside as the outside. The polished wooden floors had numerous rugs, tables and a large dresser standing around the edge while the walls had several mirrors of all shapes and sizes. A large window on the landing gave the whole place a light and airy feel. Two large sitting rooms had sofas and chairs and sitting on every surface was a tasteful vase or ornament. The heavily polished dark wood had crochet doilies to stop the sun fading the tops. Walls were adorned with pictures large and small of scenes reminding them of home. Mr Brown watched as Hannah almost pirouetted as she took in how much it could all be worth.

As though he read her thoughts, Mr Brown said, "Are you pricing everything up to sell, Mrs Phelan?" His eyes glinted with humour.

"No, no, of course not," Hannah replied, somewhat embarrassed as her cheeks flushed crimson. "I was wondering how you managed to find such wonderful items in this country. It's lovely."

"It was my wife's bartering point to get her to come here. We almost took over the hold of the ship with crates and furniture until there was almost nothing left at home. It's her to thank for making it homely but I'm afraid she hasn't settled, which is where I hope your daughter will help." He turned to Hannah. "Let me show you her room if she decides to stay."

The three of them walked up the wide staircase as it bent round to the right showing numerous doors leading off the main corridor. Mr Brown pointed to the far end where a much smaller set of stairs led to the women servants' quarters. They were led into an opulent but tasteful lady's room with a long window almost as large as the wall framing the river and out to sea.

It took in the front of the house so anyone coming or going could be seen from here. They were shown a lady's dressing room with a door to a much smaller room. In this room was a single bed, chest of drawers and a colourful rag rug on the floor. The small rectangular window looked onto a side garden and although it was a nice view there was no hint of the sea.

"This would be Amy-Rose's room so she could be close to her mistress," Mr Brown said in a matter of fact tone.

At her beck and call, Hannah thought, as Mr Brown explained his room was further down the corridor though they were not invited to look inside.

"Come," Mr Brown said, "I'll show you the rest of the downstairs rooms though my study is a bit of a mess."

Hannah gasped when she saw the library, grabbing at Daniel's arm. "Oh look at all those books," she said, wanting to run her fingers down the spine, to smell the paper, to sit in a chair and read.

"You're more than welcome to borrow one or two if you wish," Mr Brown said turning to Hannah. "Any favourite author?"

"Not really, anything would be good. I've read the bible so many times, I sometimes feel the need of something a little lighter now and then." Hannah smiled.

"Let's take a seat for a moment and discuss the business of your daughter." Mr Brown offered them the two leather chairs while he propped himself on the edge of the large desk. "Now what if I explain the contracts of the current staff and we work from there. What do you say?"

Hannah nodded uncomfortably while Daniel maintained eye contact with Mr Brown.

"Most of the staff are contracted to me. They receive time off to attend church if they wish and two days leave every three months. Most of them have nowhere to go so they usually remain here," he said in a matter of fact way.

Daniel spoke for the first time since tea. "Well Amy-Rose does have somewhere to go and I am sure I speak for Hannah, Mrs Phelan, when I say she would expect her daughter to come home to her family every weekend." He looked toward her.

"Yes, oh yes. I couldn't bear her to be away for months on end. She is still a child, my child." Hannah continued, "I don't want her to be contracted. If she isn't happy, I want her to be able to come home."

"That could be awkward as it sets a precedence which the other staff may see as preferential treatment and not take too kindly to your daughter. It would single her out so to speak," Mr Brown replied.

"The rest of the staff don't need to know and I hope you will take what steps are necessary to prevent any bad feeling. Her wages, I assume, would reflect her shorter working hours so I don't see what the problem would be?" Daniel said, sitting upright in the chair.

Hannah wasn't really interested in the money. It was her daughter's welfare which was paramount and she felt she needed to make herself clear. "Look, if my daughter and your wife get on, I will allow her to come here Monday to Friday on a daily basis until she settles, maybe a month. If at any time she is not happy with what is expected of her then she is at liberty to leave. That's all I've got to say."

"You're a tough negotiator, Mrs Phelan. I could do with you next time I have to speak to the workers on the harbour." Mr Brown held out his hand. "Let's go and speak to the ladies in question and see what has transpired. What do you say?" He didn't wait for an answer but strode over to the door, opening it widely to let his guests through.

Mrs Brown and Amy-Rose were silent as they went out onto the veranda. The girl smiled shyly when she saw her mother. Hannah's heart went out to her, wondering what was to become of her. Mr Brown temporarily disappeared, while Hannah and Daniel stood close together somewhat uncomfortably as they were not offered a seat, returning a few moments later with Kitty and Victoria just as Ned came round the corner with the cart. A large basket had been filled with the remains of the afternoon tea. Hannah tried to object but her protestations were brushed away.

"After discussing things with my wife and you with Amy-Rose. may I call in and see you next week, Mrs Phelan?" Mr Brown asked as he helped her onto the cart.

"Yes of course, that would be most acceptable," Hannah replied. She almost said she would look forward to it but that would have been too informal, as though they were friends.

The two younger girls were sent to their bedroom to put on their nightclothes before returning for a glass of milk and to tell Maggie about their trip. Hannah was a little concerned about Amy-Rose who had hardly spoken since they had left the Brown's house so she asked her to unpack the large wicker basket. It was as she was putting a few fancies on a plate for Maggie that she found her voice. "Oh look mam, there's three books at the bottom of the basket."

"What a kind man," Hannah replied and she meant it. She thought he had a twinkle in his eyes as well as a lovely voice. She bet he was a charmer with the women before he married.

Maggie took herself to her room to allow Hannah to talk to Amy-Rose alone. She began by saying that she would be happy with whatever decision she made and would always be her daughter who she loved very much.

Asking her what she thought of Mrs Brown, Amy-Rose replied, "Well she didn't say much to start with, then told me I would be expected to do whatever she asked, help her dress, do her hair, make sure her room was tidy. In the afternoon she spent some time with the children and that was when I would go into the kitchen for my lunch. There seemed so much to do, mam, I'm scared I won't be able to do it."

Hannah calmed her by telling her what she had discussed with Mr Brown and the fact that she would at the beginning at least be able to come home each day and the weekend would be free. It could be a golden opportunity to be employed in a big house, not as a servant, but as a companion. She was sure there were not many houses so large in Australia, not like England where the gentry seemed to be everywhere. In the end she hugged her daughter. "Let's sleep on it and make a decision after that. There's no rush." Kissing her eldest daughter on the top of her head, she continued, "Go on, now off to bed. I'll be up soon."

Hannah poured herself another cup of tea which was now well stewed and tepid but she sipped it anyway. What was to happen to her beautiful daughter who she knew would shortly attract all sorts of unwanted male attention? It was something she felt she could control while she was under the same roof. She should have made her welfare more clear to Mr Brown and made a mental note to mention it should Amy-Rose decide she wanted to work for them.

She thought the term was loco-parentis as that was written on the paperwork for Victoria's care.

She wished she could slip along to talk to Mary but it was too late now. Instead she picked up her shawl and went to see if Daniel was still awake. The light was lit in the kitchen so she tapped on the door before going inside. The first thing she did was burst into tears.

"You have to stop this. Hannah. Every time I see you, you start crying and that's not the first time I've said it," he laughed gently.

"What am I to do? She is but a child," Hannah asked but needing no reply.

"She would have to find work somewhere and you don't want her working in a hotel or bar, do you? Daniel said. "Let Amy-Rose make the final decision. If she doesn't want to go, that's fine and you've worried for nothing. If she does, then maybe you need to do more talking."

Hannah nodded. She knew he was right. She looked into his face. He was a handsome man in a rugged sort of way and at that moment she realised that she loved him nearly as much as he loved her. This time when he kissed her, she returned his passion. Both wanted to feel the closeness of the other as they went past the point of no return and they made love against the kitchen table. Both frantic, wanting to hold each other tightly. When their passion was sated neither spoke, there was nothing to say. Hannah smoothed down her dress, embarrassed and not sure where they went from here.

"I have to go," she said, pulling her shawl around her shoulders.

"I love you, Hannah, you know that. I have since the day I met you and I want us to be a family together." Daniel stroked her cheek with his hand.

"I know, and I love you too but I won't live with you. We have been through this before. Look, we will talk more tomorrow. Goodnight." Hannah left him standing there.

As she lay on the verge of sleep, Hannah felt a warm glow about what had happened. They were meant to be together and one day they would be. He was the only man for her and she fell asleep feeling his arms around her.

It seemed like only a few minutes before she heard the girls shuffling about, the room gave them no privacy with the four of them in two sets of bunk beds. Every move could be heard when the wood creaked as those above turned over. Getting up to sort out breakfast, Hannah felt truly content for the first time in years, in fact she was singing to herself as they all trooped down the stairs. Kitty was always chatty first thing in the morning and was more excited than ever at the thought of telling her school friends about yesterday's trip. She knew she would have no trouble with Kitty making her way in life, she didn't have the looks of her sister but had a much sunnier disposition. She was a helpful girl with plenty of friends.

Victoria joined in the chatter but was placid like her mother who Hannah talked about often. How much the child remembered she never said but seemed happy enough in the home. The two younger ones looked more like sisters and Hannah looked on Victoria as a daughter.

Amy-Rose was another kettle of fish altogether. She had the sullenness of her maternal grandfather, Hannah's father. She always felt she deserved more than she had and Hannah knew deep down she was lazy, expecting someone else to provide her with the finer things in life but didn't want to work hard to get them. Perhaps if this job offer came about it would be the best thing for her. With that thought, Hannah decided that she wouldn't stand in the girl's way if she chose to take the position.

Each child gave Hannah a kiss as she let them out of the front door. They turned at the end of the street to wave to her before entering the school gate. Maggie was collecting the breakfast pots when she returned to the kitchen. Picking up the shop keys, Hannah said, "When you're ready, come through and I'll tell you about yesterday." It was a good excuse to get her into the shop without mentioning Samuel Fletcher.

Turning the shop sign to open, Hannah looked around her little shop. She would never be rich or have a house like the Brown's but it kept a roof over their head and clothes on their back. She was also lucky to be loved by a man like Daniel who would care for her family as his own. Having afternoon tea yesterday reminded her of Primmy's tea room which gave her an idea for the future, but for now she had enough to think about with Amy-Rose and Daniel.

Maggie arrived with two cups of tea in her hand, putting them on the shop table before going into the kitchen for a chair. Once she had sat herself comfortably, she turned to Hannah. "I'm ready and I want an account of everything."

So Hannah gave her friend chapter and verse of what happened at the Brown's house and the number of staff they had everywhere, only stopping as people came into the shop. Business was brisk, people had heard the gossip, hoping to get a piece for themselves. Hannah didn't mind as long as she was making a little money, sure that people would find out what was going on soon enough.

Hannah hadn't long finished talking when the bell went again, bringing in Mary and the children. Maggie proffered her seat, saying, "Begging your pardon, I'll go next door. I don't think my ears could take another listening."

So Hannah told the story of yesterday's trip all over again although this time the listener asked many more questions and gave advice. Hannah expected no less. She explained how helpful Daniel had been. She didn't mention their coming together. She was too embarrassed to even tell Mary.

It was late morning of the Thursday before Mr Brown breezed into the shop like an old friend. After the cordial pleasantries, he said, "Well, Mrs Phelan shall we get down to the business in hand. I'm sure you have plenty to say so why don't I come straight to the point and say that your daughter charmed my wife and we would like to offer her the position of lady's maid and companion. What do you have to say?"

"Well, Mr Brown," Hannah responded in the same vein, "Amy-Rose would like to accept the position but with one or two small changes."

Hannah was about to go on when he put his hand to his head.

"Why is working with women so much more complicated. I'll never understand how they think." He gave a mock grimace.

"If you understood how a woman's mind worked, Mr Brown, life would be very dull for all of us, I'm sure." Hannah laughed and he joined in. "Now I feel, we both feel, it would be better for Amy-Rose to return home each evening for as long as it takes for her to be happy. Would there be a problem for someone to collect and return her each day, Monday to Friday?"

"Well, that wasn't what I envisaged. We did agree a month. Could we perhaps agree to two months?"

"It's not negotiable, Mr Brown. Until Amy-Rose tells me differently I want her home each evening. She is still a child, after all."

"It's a pity you couldn't go into politics, Mrs Phelan." They both laughed loudly this time. "Right then, what if we say I'll pay her five shilling a week with her lunch and uniform provided until she moves into the house, then to cover bed and board it will reduce to four shilling. After twelve months, I will review her wages and responsibility."

He held out his hand and Hannah took it. She had just agreed her daughter's short term future.

Eight weeks later, Amy-Rose finished school with her certificate and began working for the Browns the following Monday. She would be collected by Ned at eight each morning and returned at six.

The first few days Hannah worried about her, especially as she seemed to be exhausted but after a few weeks of getting into a routine Amy-Rose seemed settled. She talked each evening about her day which included helping Mrs Brown to wash. She would then lay out the day's clothes before brushing and fastening her hair with slides. Her mistress would return to sitting in a chair looking out of the window while Amy-Rose tidied the bedroom, taking the bowl of water to the closet. One of the women came in each day to remove the waste – she was given the title of 'necessary woman', she told them and they all laughed. Fancy someone who cleared away the slops having such a name, they all said in their different ways. She had left the door open to the closet one day and Mrs Brown had seen the woman removing the waste so she was told off.

"Have you made any friends?" Victoria asked when there was a pause for breath.

"No, of course not, silly. My day is with the mistress."

Victoria wouldn't be put off. "What about when you have your lunch?"

Amy-Rose put her head down. "No, I eat on my own." She didn't want to say that she was ignored by the other staff as they talked around her, as though she wasn't there, and she knew they didn't like her, she could feel it.

"Well, I wouldn't like that, to have no friends," Victoria replied.

Hannah often asked her if she was happy and she said she was fine. As Hannah finished a book Mr Brown had loaned her, she gave it to Amy-Rose to return, and another was sent back.

CHAPTER FIFTEEN
THE EVENT

Hannah's dalliance with Daniel became known as 'the event' in her mind anyway. Things happened before or after 'the event'. It remained between the two of them though neither uttered any word pertaining to it. For Hannah she knew she had passed the point of no return. One day she would be married, she would become a respectable Mrs Jerrold. She knew Daniel would always be there for her and that gave her comfort.

The shop was still doing well, the girls were happy and the extra money she had from Amy-Rose was saved so they could eventually move into a bigger house or toward her daughter's marriage. Mary was pregnant for the third time and a move to a larger place was imperative. They had looked at a number of houses but what they could afford was not suitable. The owner of the timber yard was adamant that someone needed to be on site in case of accident or emergency at night. The two young boys were deemed not old enough so that left Daniel.

Hannah wanted to protest that he couldn't move, she needed him to be near, but she couldn't voice her concerns. She would miss the closeness that the last few months had brought but perhaps it was for the best. She was worried she would be found out by Mary or Maggie.

She feared if it happened again she could become pregnant and where would that leave her. Daniel never mentioned applying for a divorce and she felt she couldn't, shouldn't ask.

So a few days later Daniel moved his personal things out of the rooms above the shop and into the flat at the timber yard. The only items of furniture he took with him were his single bed and chair.

Mary on the other hand seemed to have acquired all sorts of items. The cart was overloaded and the men struggled to get the double bed up the narrow staircase. It was almost impossible to turn the frame on the small landing. After much toing and froing it eventually scraped through the door, filling the bedroom. A single bed was made for Ruby and one for Corrine to move into once the baby needed the box Dennis had made.

The first few weeks were pandemonium with Mary and the children vying for space in the small kitchen with Hannah, while Ruby made herself a nuisance running in and out of the shop. There wasn't enough room in the kitchen for Ruby to play nor for Corrine to crawl safely let alone try to walk. Hannah was becoming exasperated with Mary who wanted to talk all the time but Hannah loved her too much to be cross with her. When Corrine fell against the stove, banging her eye, the screaming brought Maggie through to see who was being murdered and she came up with the idea of moving the shop into her front room and this would give Mary more space.

Mr Brown often called into the shop when he was in town and suggested they have a grand opening with a ribbon and someone to make a speech. Hannah told him he had just put himself forward for the role.

She was up early on the Monday morning to put the finishing touches to the new shop. It was almost twice the size of the original one once all the boxes and old furniture had been removed. She kept a small two-seater sofa positioned in the opposite corner to the front door. Hannah placed a nest of tables beside it that gave the place a homely feel. Daniel and Dennis had made her a counter standing on two packing crates which had been turned onto their sides to give her storage space underneath. The door into the kitchen finished off that wall. The small tables from the old shop had been replaced mainly by bookshelves between the sofa and the long window. She worried that the place would look empty but positioned one or two items on each shelf. The lower shelves held pots and pans and kitchen utensils. Items of jewellery sat in baskets on the counter. The final wall held pictures and mirrors of all types and conditions.

The window sparkled, now with curtains Maggie had made but Hannah wanted people to look in so placed a small vase of flowers on the sill but that was all. She did a full turn around the room and once she was satisfied with the look returned to the kitchen where Maggie was busy putting biscuits onto a baking tray. Glasses in all shapes and sizes had been retrieved from the shop and were sitting on a tray waiting to be filled with the wine Mr Brown had donated.

Hannah was nervous and excited about the new venture, not new 'per se', but she knew it gave her the opportunity to expand further.

Now the day arrived and a large crowd gathered in front of the shop to hear Mr Brown make his speech. He spoke about how the country needed people like Hannah, Mrs Phelan, entrepreneurs who would make the country grow. It didn't matter where people came from in this wonderful land, everyone was equal and people should support local enterprise. He praised the market traders and the tenacity of those living in shacks while trying to get a foothold on life.

Hannah hadn't expected it to be such a grand affair nor had she expected Mrs Brown and Amy-Rose to attend with him. Her daughter seemed to have grown in poise and was attentive to her mistress, even providing her with a chair to sit on while the speech was made. Mr Brown invited his wife to cut the ribbon and Amy-Rose helped her to her feet.

Mary was outside holding Corrine while Ruby chewed and whined, wanting to get a better view. Mr Brown picked the child up with one strong arm which startled her to silence while offering his other arm to his wife. Amy-Rose followed behind as Maggie stood just inside the shop, holding the tray of wine. Mr Brown took a glass as did the others who followed behind.

Hannah desperately wanted to hug her daughter but instead brushed her hand as she walked past telling her she was very proud.

Mrs Brown picked up one or two trinkets passing them to Amy-Rose to take to the counter. This encouraged others to do the same and Hannah made more in one afternoon than she had done in the last month. She didn't get a chance to thank the Browns as they left shortly after, leaving Amy-Rose behind.

Mrs Brown had asked Amy-Rose to stay the week leading up to Christmas to help with the preparations and Hannah reluctantly agreed. She found it surprising that over the weeks she had become closer to Kitty who seemed to have grown up without her realising it. She had her heart set on becoming a teacher which made Hannah very happy.

Hannah, Daniel and the girls had been invited to the Browns on the last Saturday before Christmas when they were holding a party for friends and colleagues. Hannah agonised over whether to buy presents, unaware of protocol. In the end she baked another batch of lavender biscuits, which had gone down well at her shop opening, and gingerbread men for the children.

Daniel hadn't wanted to go. He had too much work on, he told her, only relenting when she told him it was an afternoon affair and if he didn't go then neither would they and that would disappoint the girls. Relenting, he said he had nothing to wear. Hannah laughed saying that was her line. She really didn't want to go, she felt a fraud, but Kitty and Victoria were so excited. Mr Brown had been incredibly kind to her and her family so felt obliged to him to attend.

Since moving and with Christmas coming up, Hannah kept the shop open later during the week but still closed at two on a Saturday. This would give her a couple of hours to get cleaned up and ready for the party.

In no time at all the cart arrived and the girls were quick to climb aboard. Hannah had wrapped the biscuits in a cloth, placing them in a basket, but holding the handle wasn't the reason her foot missed the step, nor why her mouth fell open. It wasn't Ned driving the cart but Samuel Fletcher, with a leer on his face as he looked her up and down that put the fear of God into her.

Daniel said nothing, although he knew who the man was. He

pulled at his shirt collar trying to find some breathing space, but it was Samuel Fletcher who spoke first.

"This is a nice family outing, I must say. Bet you were surprised when you saw me, Mrs Phelan? Learnt all I know about horses from your father."

"You're talking rubbish, man." Daniel looked directly at him. "I've known Mrs Phelan for years and her father never worked with horses so would you keep your ramblings to yourself. I have warned you before."

"Aye, you might have done but I never forget a face and one day we will all learn the truth about Mrs Phelan." He was shocked when Daniel grabbed the reins.

"Now listen to me, if you've anything to say about Mrs Phelan then get yourself along to the polis and tell them what you know. They can decide what action to take, otherwise keep your mouth shut. You're making a fool of yourself." Daniel was almost standing next to the man but calmed himself when he remembered the children were sitting behind him.

"Might just do that and then we can get to the bottom of what happened to her first husband. Do you remember him? Thomas Cloverley?" Samuel Fletcher replied, taking the reins and setting the horse into a trot.

"Think on. Mrs Phelan is a friend of Mr Brown and you could be out of a job if he finds you have been slandering her for no good reason, so let's hear no more about it," Daniel said more calmly.

Hannah hadn't said a word. What could she say? At every turn this man seemed to turn up and spoil things for her. It was obvious he knew something, that she knew for certain but she didn't know why he hadn't shown his hand and gone to the polis before now. Worse was how he kept cropping up when she was thinking he had disappeared. What he was planning she didn't know, couldn't know nor could she ask him. She wanted to go home but took the girls hands in hers as they turned into the drive.

Waiters resplendent in waistcoats welcomed the visitors who had arrived in all sorts of carriages, carts and landaus. She didn't get the chance to check the girls, as they jumped off the cart almost before it came to a halt, rushing up the steps. Daniel took the basket from her as he helped her step more sedately than she climbed up.

"Just let me know when you want to return," Samuel Fletcher said. "I'll be ready and waiting," he sneered.

Hannah didn't have time to think about him when Mr Brown welcomed them, shaking both their hands warmly. "Kitty and Victoria have already made themselves at home and gone off to the nursery. I should apologise in advance as they will probably be sick with all the treats laid on for them." He laughed as he passed the proffered basket to one of the servants.

Even though the seasons were the wrong way round and no one had ever seen snow in this country, the hallway looked very festive. It wasn't decked with holly but other greenery which was festooned up the staircase and along the balustrade. In the corner was a tree, the biggest Hannah had ever seen indoors, decked out with Christmas decorations. The lower branches were laden with small parcels tied with ribbon while the higher branches had tasteful silver and gold baubles. Underneath were even more parcels, the like Hannah could never imagine.

"Oh Daniel, isn't it beautiful," she said, momentarily forgetting Samuel Fletcher.

"Wonder how they got it into the house. Bet it took plenty of staff huffing and puffing," he replied, watching others come into the hallway.

"Don't be miserable. Come on, everyone seems to be going this way. Let's try and forget about what happened earlier," Hannah said without much conviction.

She spotted Amy-Rose standing behind a chair where Mrs Brown was accepting compliments before they moved away toward the garden. Mrs Brown shook their hands, telling Amy-Rose to take her break and go with her mother to find some drinks. Moving to the front of the chair, Amy-Rose bobbed her knee before turning to her mother.

Taking her daughter's hand in hers they looked for somewhere to sit but all the seats around the garden seemed to be taken so they walked slowly talking generally. It didn't seem more than a few minutes before the girl said she would have to get back to her mistress. "I'll see you later, mam."

Hannah was about to kiss her but thought better of it. Although only fourteen, Amy-Rose had grown up enormously since she had been in the Brown's household. She was more assured, confident and seemed happy for which Hannah was incredibly proud.

Daniel stood by the long window that was opened into the garden where people seemed to be mingling. They all seemed to know each other as they circulated, laughing and talking in small groups before they moved on. It was like some hypnotic dance from which they were excluded.

Hannah turned to Daniel. "What am I going to do about Samuel Fletcher? What if he goes to the polis?"

"He won't. He would have to explain why he hadn't gone to them before. No, he likes to think he has a hold over you and you are letting him. Forget about him, Hannah, then he can't get to you," Daniel said in a matter of fact way.

"That's easy for you to say. I feel threatened every time I see him and he frightens me. I just want to run away," Hannah replied.

"I've told you before, ignore him. If he had anything on you, he would have shown his hand before now and he hasn't. We can't harass the man without cause. Just don't play into his hands."

"He does know about me, he told Adam and he wants to marry me. I've told you all that before." Hannah felt exasperated at Daniel's seeming lack of concern.

Hannah hadn't expected Daniel to respond in that manner though she knew deep down he was probably right. She was about to suggest they return to the garden when the Browns walked into the room with Amy-Rose close behind.

They walked toward the ornamental fireplace where it looked as though a fire had never been set. Mrs Brown took a seat as Mr Brown called for quiet as he began the event with, "Those of you who expected music and dancing, get back to England!"

People laughed and some joker piped up, "We could adjourn to the hotel, I think they have all that's required for entertainment."

Again there was much laughter where another voice called, "You should know, most of your money is spent in there, so I'm told." This time there was a titter around the room as people looked to the man who had spoken.

"Come now, gentlemen, there are ladies present somewhere," Mr Brown said to more laughter. "It's my dear wife to thank for this, she wanted to bring the old country to this God forsaken place." There was applause as Mr Brown raised his hand. "Enjoy our hospitality. There is business to be arranged here today so talk to people, let's get this country moving." Mr Brown bowed to rapturous applause as Hannah heard the gentleman next to her say, "Is that a Governor's political speech?" but she didn't hear the response.

Hannah turned to Daniel. "Shall we get the girls and sneak off? I feel so out of place here, and dowdy in my Sunday dress. All the women are dressed up to the nines."

"Fishing for compliments are you? No one here could hold a candle to you. Whatever you wear you will always be the best to me. Oh, too late, we've been spotted."

Mr Brown breezed over with what Hannah would describe as a portly gentleman whose silver tunic buttons were straining to remain fastened. He had a row of sweat close to his hairline but seemed not to notice. He was chatting to Mr Brown as though they knew each other well.

"Mr Jerrold, Mrs Phelan, may I introduce a good friend of mine, Captain Munroe." They shook his warm limp hand cordially before Mr Brown continued. "The Captain here is responsible for bringing the trains over from England as well as being an astute business man. His wife deals in antiques and often buys up boxes of unknown quality at house auctions around the home counties. Well anyway why don't you take a stroll around the garden to see if you can be mutually beneficial to each other." With that Mr Brown left the three of them looking at each other.

Captain Munroe proffered his arm which Hannah reluctantly took, Daniel walking the other side of her. "Gabriel tells me you have an emporium selling all sorts of 'objet d'art'?"

"Well I would hardly say that. It's basically a second hand shop where I sell anything I think can make a profit." Hannah wrinkled her nose at the stale odour coming from the man.

"My wife deals in antiques which she often purchases through house sales and sometimes buys lots where only one or two items are suitable. The rest she stores in boxes. What does she do with them, I ask you, madam?"

"I've no idea?" Hannah said, wishing she could get rid of this tiresome man.

"Well Gabriel thought of you. What do you say?" Captain Munroe asked.

Daniel interrupted as Hannah was about to speak. "Well if you don't think they'll sell for much in England, what makes you think a profit could be made here, sir?"

"No, you misunderstand me, sir. My wife has to pay the auctioneer a percentage in a selling fee and that cuts out much of any profit. If you agreed to buy, say ten boxes at five pounds per box, I could ship them here for free."

"Fifty pounds? That's a lot of money when I have no idea of the size or content of the boxes, sir." Hannah replied.

"Sometimes in business you have to take a gamble, am I right?" Captain Munroe now looked at Daniel or affirmation.

"I'm not so naïve, sir, as to risk mine and my family's livelihood on a whim." With that Hannah turned toward the house. She had heard enough of this pompous man.

Not to be put off, Captain Munroe said, "Well perhaps I can call into your shop in the New Year before I set sail to discuss the matter further, when you have had more time to think it over?"

"As you wish, sir, though I am sure that my answer will be the same," Hannah replied. "I bid you good day."

After they had gone their separate ways, Daniel spoke to her quietly. "I could lend you some of the money if you think it's a good idea."

"Thank you but as the Captain said, I need time to think about it. Now do you think we can leave as I don't feel comfortable." Hannah made to move but Daniel put his hand on her arm.

"We can't just wander round the house looking for Kitty and

Victoria so let's head toward the hall and see if we can find Amy-Rose or one of the many servants so they can go and get them."

Hannah followed Daniel around the edge of the room. No one seemed to notice them hugging the wall as they passed the many talking loudly, sipping wine from crystal glasses. As Daniel had said, there were as many staff as guests and they soon found a young man who disappeared up the staircase to get the children.

While waiting, Hannah said, "I should never have come. I don't belong in a place or company like this. I don't know why we were invited."

"I was only invited along to accompany you, so I've had a great day," Daniel said, pulling at his collar again, laughing and so did Hannah as the girls came rushing down the stairs.

"Do we have to go, mam?" Kitty said. "We were having a lovely time playing games."

"Yes," said Victoria, not to be outdone. "I haven't tried all the sweets yet." They both begged, hanging on to Hannah's dress.

"No, come on, we don't want to outstay our welcome. What if we walk up to Arthur's Point to look at the sea? We might see a ship setting sail."

They hurried down the drive as though they were being chased. They hadn't even said goodbye to Amy-Rose but it was too late now.

Instead of turning left at the gate to go into town, they turned right with the girl's running on ahead. "What did you make of that?" Hannah said, not waiting for a reply. "I just feel the whole thing was a set up and fifty pounds is a lot of money to hand over to a stranger."

"Yes, you are right, of course, but try and think about it without any emotion. You're annoyed at the moment and that clouds your judgement," Daniel said calmly.

"I know, I know, but what a cheek and as usual you are right. Why are you always so objective about everything, that's what I'd like to know." Hannah laughed.

"Probably because I'm always right." Daniel set off to chase the girls and Hannah followed laughing loudly.

They all dropped to the ground, red faced from the exertion and the slight sea breeze was welcome as they tried to catch their breath. Hannah wondered why they didn't come up here more often. The view was wonderful, looking at the changing colour of the sea the deeper it got. They could see the jetty jutting out with ships lined up on both sides.

Next time I'll bring a picnic, Hannah thought, as she sat staring out to sea, keeping half an eye on the girls who were picking pretty yellow flowers.

Amy-Rose came home on Christmas Eve, remaining until 2nd January 1885. Everyone was busy and the house had hardly room to move. Hannah had put a garland of greenery on the windowsill of the shop to give it a festive feel. Maggie proved to be excellent with a needle and thread making all the girl's stockings with their names embroidered on, though she did concede to just put Amy on Amy-Rose's as her fingers were sore. Hannah had purchased some pretty green material to make a dress for Amy-Rose and for hair adornment using a drawstring through a length of material. Hannah made rag dolls out of waste material for Mary's girls. The dress was an extravagance Hannah knew but Amy-Rose tipped up her money each week and it was saved in the hope that it would pay for her eldest daughter's eventual marriage.

Daniel arrived at around one o'clock when they all squeezed around the table, all ten of them, though Ruby sat on her mother's knee and Corrine sat in her pram.

Hannah had never had a big family Christmas until she came to Australia. As a child, it would be just her and her mam. Her dad usually slept off a skinful from the night before so they had to be quiet. They never had an invite to someone else's Christmas but her mam tried her best. What would her mother think if she could see her now, with the smiling happy faces and the laughter all around the table. Just for a moment, and it was just a moment, she felt melancholy.

CHAPTER SIXTEEN

ONE EVENT AFTER ANOTHER

Feeling surplus to requirements, Hannah decided to open the shop in the hope it would take her mind off things. She had only just cleared away the Christmas items, dusted the windowsill and damp wiped the book shelves and the floor by wrapping the cloth around the brush when the door burst open.

Without any formalities, Captain Munroe said, "Have you thought about my offer? I'll be sailing later so need an answer."

"And a Happy New Year to you, sir, I'm sure," Hannah replied. "I have decided not to take you up on your offer this time but I thank you for your consideration."

"Well, you won't get an offer like that every day you know," he blustered.

"My decision is made so I bid you good day and a safe passage home."

"You'll regret it, madam. I could have made you a small fortune and I won't be offering again," Captain Munroe said angrily.

"Is that a threat, Captain Munroe? I will have to speak to Mr Brown about the company he keeps. Now good day, sir!" Hannah moved toward the door to let him out. She didn't like that man, his whole manner was rude bordering on aggression.

Letting out a deep sigh as he left, she was relieved to see Maggie coming through from the kitchen.

"Well done, I was just about to come through and put my boot up his backside!" Maggie said.

"Where on earth did you hear such language?" Hannah burst out laughing.

"I don't like men who think they can bully women. As my Jack, God rest his soul, used to say, men like that need a taste of their own medicine. We could do with a drop of the hard stuff but I've only got tea though we could have a snifter and pretend it's whisky." Maggie patted Hannah's hand.

It was the first time Hannah had seen Maggie let her guard drop although she seemed to get on better with Mary. They would often sit in the yard together, watching Ruby play.

Gabriel Brown was the only other person to call into the shop that day. He breezed in, making Hannah smile at his easy manner. "Happy New Year to you and your family, Mrs Phelan. You left the party early. I hope it wasn't because of anything you heard?" he said.

"And a Happy New Year to you, Mr Brown. Yes, we left early,. I felt out of place. So what was it I shouldn't have heard?" Hannah replied.

"Oh you know how men like to brag, especially when they've had a drink, most of it speculative, to see how others react. How did you get on with Captain Munroe?"

"I'm sure you are already aware, Mr Brown, I turned his offer down as I wasn't sure of the authenticity of the goods, if that's the right word?" Hannah responded.

"You must do as you see fit, Mrs Phelan," he said rather tartly. "I have called in to talk about Amy-Rose and pass this on to you." He handed Hannah a piece of paper which she looked at briefly. "Now this is something I wholeheartedly recommend if you have any funds available. It's a land sale. I can tell you now land will more than double in the next few years what with the railway and harbour."

Hannah hadn't really been listening but asked, "What about Amy-Rose? She's not in trouble, is she?"

"No, no, on the contrary, my wife seems much happier now she has someone to talk to. No, it's the daily trip I want to discuss. We did say we would look at the arrangements." Mr Brown nodded.

"I'll talk to my daughter, Mr Brown, and if she is happy then so am I," Hannah replied.

It was agreed that Amy-Rose would live in the Brown's household during the week and the girl seemed happy with the decision, making Hannah less troubled about any contact with Samuel Fletcher.

It was the following day before Hannah looked at the leaflet for the sale of land and it gave a long discussion around the table. She took herself off to the Land Agent's office for the list of land to be sold but it was the Sunday afternoon before they all took a stroll to look at what was available.

Leading up to the auction she had worried about spending so much money, while telling herself it was too good an opportunity for her family. Now she not only had her own business but perhaps a share in land. Who would have thought it, certainly not Hannah.

Two weeks later Hannah counted, re-counted and counted again the money she had to buy the land. She had never seen so much in all her life and was worried about being in charge of her friends' life savings. Putting it into separate money bags, she wrote how much she could bid on each piece of land on a piece of paper.

The bags she placed into her coat pocket, keeping her hand over the opening so it didn't fall out. Any thief would know exactly where to find it but she didn't know what else to do. Finding herself right at the front of the growing crowd, feeling conspicuous, she moved toward the back but worried she wouldn't hear the auctioneer once he got started. Her hands were damp with anticipation as she moved to the side. Looking around she seemed to be the only woman on her own. There were one or two others but they were stood with who she assumed were their husbands. Nodding to one or two she listened to the conversation of four men at the right hand side of her. She wasn't sure if they were government land agents here to push up the price, which would be bad news for her. They could be bidding on behalf of someone wanting to keep their business quiet but she would never know.

Moving from one foot to the other, Hannah thought it was strange to have the auction outside the hotel. She was already feeling warm. The auctioneer banged his gavel on the wooden stand making her jump, but also a horse reared up behind the crowd almost upending the rider.

The bidding set off at a fast and furious pace, prices going for far more than Hannah could afford and she was beginning to feel she had wasted her day. However by the time they got to the final page of plots, the two Hannah was interested in, most people seemed to have spent their money. She had learnt over the years of buying lots for the shop not to show her hand too early. The price slowly increased before it stalled. Hannah lifted her hand twice before the gavel fell and it was hers. Now all she needed to do was hold her nerve and purchase the corner plot next to it. She knew how much money she had left, eventually getting it just under her maximum price.

The auctioneer's clerk sat at a table just inside the hotel bar where he watched her shaking hands count out the money in turn for each piece of land. She had never spent that much in one go, ever and it was a mixture of euphoria and a sick feeling that she had used up all her savings.

Her purse was so much lighter as she walked home with the paperwork for the two pieces of land. The smaller piece was for Victoria, using the money her father had left for her. Hannah thought even if Adam returned one day, he would be able to build a home for them both, and if not, well it was a sort of legacy for the child. What remaining money was left, and there wasn't a great deal, Hannah would keep for when Victoria was older.

The other plot of land was larger, large enough to build a pair of homes, one for Mary, Dennis and family as well as Maggie who would live with them. The other for Hannah, Daniel and the girls. The purchase had been a collective as this was the only way they would have been able to afford it even with the money Hannah had from the sale of her house and land.

The plot was nowhere as big as the one she had bought with Mickey years ago but it was much closer to town being toward Arthur's Point and looking onto the river inlet.

The agreement was that they would build for Dennis and Mary first as their ever increasing family was cramped into the small house which belonged to Daniel. As soon as they had enough money to buy the wood they would begin at weekends and evenings when they could.

Hannah had heard nothing from Dan, John or even Adam for over a year. The latter she didn't care about but she missed letters from the others. John would always keep her up to date with her friends in Northend, though she was sure Annie must be dead by now.

Hannah wrote to Dan three or four times a year. She had written to him last October wishing him season's greeting and also birthday wishes. She always tried to keep her letters light and happy with news of everyone, especially his sisters. He would be nineteen now and a young man, but she couldn't picture him other than that surly boy who had lived with her for such a short time. Although it had been a tremendous wrench to let him go, his occasional letters told her he was happy so she was surprised when Mrs Coyle came into the shop with a large packet for her.

Hannah's first reaction was to rip the envelope open but Mrs Coyle stood waiting to see what it was and Hannah didn't want to share the news, whatever it was, with her so placed it on the shop counter, thanking her for being so good bringing it. The woman left, annoyed that she had been dismissed without knowing what was in the package.

Putting the closed sign on the door, Hannah ripped the envelope open, the letter from Dan told her he was second in command on a ship running between Portsmouth and New York, but it was what else he told her that shook her. The enclosed envelope was for Daniel but she couldn't wait until he returned from work to tell the others, rushing into the kitchen and into the yard to Mary and Maggie.

"I've got a letter from Dan," she said waving the paper at them. "You'll never guess what he's said?"

They both looked at her but didn't speak as Hannah continued, "Adele's dead! She's been dead about a year and no one thought to let us know."

As usual it was Mary who made the point. "Well they would hardly tell you but someone should have informed Daniel, after all he is still her husband. There's nothing stopping you naming the day now, is there?" She laughed.

Ignoring her, Hannah said, "There's a letter here for Daniel. I don't know whether it's her will but it seems quite bulky. Dan said she left him the coal business as he was the closest to family but he doesn't want it. He thinks Daniel should have it as he was the one who built it up. Oh, just think, we could all go home." Hannah became excited.

"Don't get ahead of yourself. It will be up to Daniel what he does and you don't know what's in his letter yet," Mary said, putting a damper on Hannah's excitement.

She could hardly wait for the evening as she rushed off to talk to Daniel about what was in his letter. He said nothing as he studied the paperwork, turning it backwards and forwards as he took it in. Hannah was desperate to know what was going on but said nothing while he perused the legalities.

"Well," he said, "that's a turn up. Adele left everything to Dan, the coal business, furniture and money. The business is doing well. She seems to have made a success of that but the solicitor has made it clear that as her husband, even though she wrote a will, I'm next of kin." He seemed melancholy.

"So what are you going to do?"

"I need to think. It's a bit of a shock after all this time."

"What's there to think about? We could all go home," Hannah stated quietly.

"Go home? Oh Hannah, no, I could never go home. I couldn't face the journey. Would you really want to go back when you've just bought land?" Daniel asked.

"That could be sold to pay for the passage. If we sold everything, we could all go home. It wouldn't be like before. We would have a cabin, it would be like a holiday." Hannah became animated.

"Have you mentioned this to Mary? What about the girls? They were born here. You wouldn't be able to take Victoria," Daniel replied.

"I've a letter saying she is my ward, so why couldn't I take her?" Hannah was incredulous that Daniel seemed to be able to find so many obstacles in the way.

"I don't know, I just don't know. We've made a life here. If I sold it all, I could buy a share in the timber yard, build a house, so many things the money could help with. I'll need to let the solicitor know what I want to do but I can't think. Oh Hannah, don't look like that. It's a big decision for all of us, not just for you, and I'm not going to make it without going into it all so let's change the subject." He took her hand.

It was too late to talk to Mary so Hannah lay in bed trying to understand Daniel's reluctance to go home. Her journey had been so much worse than his but she would go through it in a blink of an eye. Perhaps if she could get everyone else on her side, he would give in, surely he would. Maybe then if she was in England she would get to see Dan sometimes. After all, it seemed he had found time to visit Adele over the years, according to his letter. She couldn't sleep for thinking about this being a fresh start for them all.

The following morning Hannah had hardly closed the door after seeing the girls off to school when Mary waddled into the kitchen with Corrine. She would give birth to her third child in the next few days, Hannah was sure.

"What did Daniel have to say about his letter?" Mary asked, flopping uncomfortably on a chair.

Hannah explained to both Mary and Maggie what was in the letter and also that it could be an opportunity to return home to a business.

"Would you go back? You've done so well here," Mary asked.

"We could all go back. Don't you see?" Hannah replied. "It could be a new start for all of us."

"We couldn't. Dennis isn't allowed to return to England, him being Irish, and my life wasn't up to much," Mary stated.

"What do you mean? You've never mentioned this before." Hannah looked at Mary.

"Well it never came up before. Dennis said it was because of the Irish uprising but I don't know, you would have to ask him," Mary told her.

"I'd miss you all if you went," Maggie joined in.

"I thought you would come back with us?"

"Oh no, my Jack's buried here and I want to be with him, when, you know, I go to my maker," Maggie told Hannah.

"Well that's it then. I can't go without you so we all stay." Hannah was disappointed. It wasn't the outcome she expected at all. She wanted to cry but didn't really know why. Deep down she had always felt that one day she would return to Northend, to somehow prove she was innocent of the crime she had been convicted of. But what about the one she had so far got away with, if she returned to England would she be found out? It was no good thinking about being closer to Dan, she couldn't leave the rest of them behind. Daniel had got his way without a fight and she would just have to get on with it, no matter how disappointed she felt.

She didn't get chance to find out what Daniel intended to do as Mary went into labour in the early hours of the following morning. Dennis banged on the back door for her before he ran for the woman who dealt in births and Rory O'Reilly was born on 31 July 1884, kicking and screaming.

Everyone was delighted that they finally had a son but when Hannah asked if this would be the last, Mary smiled and said she hoped not. Hannah was grateful for the distraction of a new baby but felt deflated at the thought of never going home. She would have to stop calling it home as this was her home even though at times it didn't feel like it.

With the urgency to build Dennis and Mary's house, the men worked every evening and weekend they could. Even the two young lads and one or two of the Irish friends helped out at times.

Hannah was past herself wondering what Daniel was going to do with his business and monies from England. When she heard Dennis return later on the Sunday evening, she put the plated meal into her basket, making her excuses to take it along to Daniel.

Knocking on the flat door, she went in without waiting for a response. Daniel stood with his shirt off, washing himself at the sink, his back toward her. The weals never failed to shock her. He half turned to acknowledge her but continued with his ablutions before drying himself, rubbing his hands through his hair before speaking.

"This is a nice surprise. I thought I was going to have a piece of dry bread for my supper yet here you are, like an angel."

Hannah smiled. "How are you?"

"Tired. You?"

"Yes, I'm fine." Her voice belayed her words.

"You're not still upset about not going home, are you? If you're really set on going then we'll go but it's not much fun carrying coal in the rain and snow." Daniel took her in his arms.

"I'll be fine," Hannah said. She had thought the homesickness would eventually pass and she could live with that but a child leaving, never to be seen again remained a gnawing ache in her heart.

"I know you're dying to ask me what I'm going to do so I'll save you the trouble and tell you that I'm going to go to the bank to see if I can get a loan against the monies from Adele and get our house built as soon as possible. What do you think? If I build you a home fit for a queen, will you marry me, Hannah Phelan?"

"What, what did you say?" she mocked him.

"Come on, woman, answer me. Will you marry me?" He hugged her tightly, his skin still damp.

"Oh Daniel, of course I'll marry you." Hannah held him close, taking in the scent of the soap on his skin.

One thing led to another and they made love with a passion they had never experienced before, totally and utterly as one. They lay entwined on his single bed for a long while before Hannah spoke, "Why don't you wait until you get the money instead of paying interest?"

"Why do women always spoil the moment by talking?" Daniel kissed the nape of her neck making her skin tingle.

"Women? How many women have spoilt your moment? Perhaps I'll have to think again about your proposal." Hannah turned to him, not waiting for an answer as they made love again more gently this time.

It was about time, Hannah thought, she really would marry for love this time.

The following Sunday evening they all sat around the kitchen table when Daniel made the announcement, though how Hannah had managed not to say anything earlier was beyond her.

"Amy-Rose, I've asked your mother to marry me and as the eldest I'm asking for your permission for us to name a date. Is that acceptable to you?" Daniel winked at her.

She liked that fact that she was being treated as an adult but said, "Kitty, Victoria, what do we say?"

"Yes, yes," they all cheered.

"Well with the decision made, we've waited long enough, so when is it to be, Mrs Phelan?" Daniel asked.

"Let's wait until the house is built and start our new life there, what do you say?" Hannah took his hand. She didn't want her married life to start in the flat with a single bed nor here with a house that was already overfull.

CHAPTER SEVENTEEN

IT NEVER RAINS BUT IT POURS

Hannah surprised everyone including herself that she seemed in no hurry to marry but as she had waited all this time, she really wanted to start married life properly so no date had yet been set. Life continued as normal, Daniel remaining in the small flat at the timber yard while Mary was trying to pack for the move to the new house, which was almost finished, and it looked so spacious after the rooms next door.

Hannah's house would have the same floor space but she wanted one huge room downstairs with a kitchen dining room at one end and a living area at the other. Every room would look out onto the river where she hoped a cool breeze would flow through in the summer. The veranda would also look to the river where she hoped she could sit and watch the world go by if she ever found time. Upstairs would have two large bedrooms with windows again looking over the river. The younger girls didn't want cramped rooms and they were happy to share so they could gossip while in bed.

She was looking forward to Amy-Rose coming home for the weekend so was surprised when the girl rushed into the shop and up the stairs to her room without a word. Locking the shop door, she followed her, tapping gently on the door before going in. Amy-Rose was laid on the bed sobbing. Hannah held her asking what was wrong, was she in trouble?

"No, I hope I'm not in trouble. It's that man Samuel Fletcher," Amy-Rose said, sitting up, showing the bodice of her dress which had been torn.

"What's happened and what's he got to do with it?" Hannah was alarmed.

"He grabbed me on the way home, trying to kiss me. He laughed when I pulled away. He said he was going to marry me and you wouldn't stop it. You won't let make me marry him, will you, please mam, he's horrible and he's old." Amy-Rose started crying again.

"Over my dead body will you marry that man. I thought I told you to keep away from him."

"He brought me back in the cart because Ned couldn't. Oh mam, it was awful, his hands were all over me. I can't go back with him, I really can't."

"No, that's alright, I can take you back on Monday but listen don't mention this to anyone, get yourself sorted. Come on, it will be alright," Hannah said, not altogether convinced.

Hannah spent the weekend worrying about what would happen to her daughter who was very quiet. It was one thing that man trying to hurt her but she was never going to let him touch her daughters.

It was the Sunday evening before Hannah got to the bottom of exactly what had gone on. Dennis had mentioned that Daniel was in bed with a fever and hadn't been in work the day before.

Plating up a dinner, Hannah went off to the timber yard. The bottom door was unlocked so she pushed the bolt in the lock before heading up the steps. She called out, "Daniel, it's only me. I've brought you something to eat."

He came out of the bedroom looking dishevelled. His skin had a grey pallor which disturbed her, but what disturbed her more was the wound by his jaw and down his neck.

"What's happened? You look terrible," Hannah said alarmingly.

"Thanks, could you boil some water? I need to clean this up." He winced as he touched his skin.

"Here eat your food while I wait for the kettle." Hannah looked at him. There was a sheen of sweat on his skin. He looked defeated, weary, she didn't know what the word was. Trying to keep the conversation going, she continued, "Has this anything to do with Amy-Rose?"

"Has she spoken to you about Samuel Fletcher?" Daniel winced as Hannah tried to clean his wound with a wet cloth.

"Yes, but I want to know how you got this?" Hannah looked at the wound which seemed to have quickly become infected. "Start talking, Mr Jerrold, this is going to hurt."

Flinching, he tried to talk through gritted teeth. "He was in the bar drinking, telling anyone who would listen that he would soon have a young wife. He was going to force himself on this girl so she would agree to the marriage. He was bragging about the mother being witless enough to give up her daughter to save her neck."

Hannah couldn't believe what she was hearing, that man would do that to a young girl, a child, her child.

Daniel continued, "Oh he was clever, never mentioning any names but I listened long enough to realise he was talking about Amy-Rose."

"Oh dear God, my poor girl. She's like a lamb to the slaughter. It can't happen, I won't let it happen, Daniel," Hannah cried.

"As I left the hotel, his horse and cart was tied up outside. It was stupid I know but I thought I would hide in the back and catch him on the road to the house."

"This needs stitching. You should see a doctor," Hannah said, trying not to think of that man, Samuel Fletcher.

"No, it doesn't. The puss needs to come out, just make it as clean as you can. There's clean strapping." He nodded to a small cupboard.

Strapping up the wound as best she could, she wrapped the material around Daniel's head and neck to keep it attached. She felt hysterical, wanting to scream at the thought of her daughter being in danger because of her. "Go on, what happened next?"

"I waited until the cart turned up the road, managing to get behind him, punching him hard on the back of the head. The horse stopped and we traded punches until he pulled out a hoof pick, lunging at me. I tried to grab his arm but as we fell forward the horse bolted and I fell off the back. He was dragged along. I didn't go and check on him. I just staggered home." Daniel put his head back, eyes closed. "I'm sorry, Hannah, I think I've made things worse."

Although, she said, "Don't worry," she was worried. "You need to get some sleep. Come down and bolt the bottom door behind me. I'll come back tomorrow and see how you are."

"What about Amy-Rose?" he asked.

"I'll take her up to the house myself," Hannah said with more confidence than she felt.

Hannah asked Amy-Rose to explain again what had happened pulling her daughter to her, hugging her tightly, but didn't tell her about Daniel's fight with Samuel Fletcher. By the time they got to the gates of the Browns' home, Hannah knew something was amiss. There were a number of polis searching the undergrowth while staff seemed to be rushing around more than usual. Hannah turned to Amy-Rose saying, "Say nothing about what happened on Friday. I'll try to speak to Mr Brown."

Amy-Rose went up the stairs to her mistress' room while Hannah stopped one of the staff asking to speak to Mr Brown.

"He's with the polis at the moment," the young lady informed her.

"What's happened?" Hannah asked with a feeling of dread in the pit of her stomach.

"One of the men is dead, that's all we've been told. Do you want to wait?"

Hannah's stomach rolled, she just knew who it was. She should be happy that the man was dead and couldn't hurt her any more but she had to get to Daniel to warn him. "No, it's alright, I just wanted to make sure my daughter, Miss Phelan, arrived safely."

She wanted to run, run as fast as she could, but didn't want to draw attention to herself, walking quickly until she reached the edge of town. Instead of going to the shop and hoping not to be seen, she headed to the timber yard. Getting no reply from Daniel's door, she spoke to the blacksmith and his assistant but they hadn't seen him and assumed he was out though as his horse and cart were still in the stable.

She didn't want to leave a note or message and instead went to the shop where she struggled to concentrate. Daniel had fought with that man so had he killed him? Would he have told her if he had? She thought not. She was getting ahead of herself. She didn't know for sure that it was Samuel Fletcher but her instinct said it was especially as no cart had turned up to collect Amy-Rose.

The day dragged on as she listened to Mary and Maggie talking but she didn't want to say anything that could incriminate Daniel or even her.

It was only after Dennis returned from work, telling them that Daniel had been arrested that panic set in. It was too late to visit him now but Hannah knew they would have to get a story straight. She had to talk to Daniel, she just had to.

After a sleepless night, Hannah presented herself at the gaol. Not only did it remind her of the time she had bailed Daniel out at Stainsby another life ago, but she had to go through the gates of what had been the correction facility at Cheapside where she started her life in Australia.

He already looked a defeated man as Hannah's heart went out to him. Whatever he had done was for her family and it was her job to get him out of this mess.

"What have they said to you?" she asked.

"That he's dead and it's my fault. Oh Hannah, I'll hang for this." Daniel couldn't go on.

"No, you won't. It's not your fault. You have to listen to me," she replied.

"His dying words were my name, he made sure." Daniel began to cry.

"Listen to me," Hannah whispered so no one other than Daniel could hear her. "You have to tell the truth."

He had a puzzled look on his face but she continued, "You fought with him at the side of the hotel but after he stabbed you, well, you went home, didn't you?" Hannah took his hand. "Daniel, look at me. You went home, didn't you?"

He nodded, confused.

"I brought you a meal so you were with me, that's what you have to say. You were with me, Daniel," Hannah said sharply.

"The judge won't believe me," Daniel said defeated.

"Yes he will, you've got to tell him. What's wrong with you?" Hannah was shocked that he seemed to have given up to his fate.

Suddenly it was time for her to leave but as she stood, she grabbed his hand. "Stick to the truth and I'll stand in the witness box and so will Amy-Rose. Be strong, Daniel. After all this we've a wedding to organise."

She kept walking, back straight, until she got through the gates before putting her hands to her face, groaning long and hard. She couldn't go back to the shop, she couldn't answer all the questions so instead walked past the new railway station, the school, her shoulders sagging under the weight of worry over Daniel's mental state.

Hannah tried to find someone to represent Daniel in defence but it seemed the lawyers all believed he was guilty. The polis would have someone for the prosecution and if no one would stand for him, it would be the hangman's noose. She couldn't, wouldn't let that happen.

It was something Mary said which gave Hannah an idea and here she was Tuesday evening back at the Brown's with Dennis. She sat explaining to Mr Brown how Samuel Fletcher had made her life a misery for years and how he had attacked Amy-Rose. His final act against her was to name Daniel as his killer, but Daniel, while not denying having had a fight with the man had certainly left him very much alive.

Mr Brown asked to speak to Amy-Rose who confirmed what her mother had said.

"I'm not sure what you want me to say?" he said.

"Well, I thought you could speak to the judge, explain. He would listen to you," Hannah said.

"I really can't get involved. A man has died and as far as we know the perpetrator has been arrested. You have to let the justice system make the decision," Mr Brown explained.

"The polis won't look for anyone else, you know that. Daniel isn't denying they fought but that was on the Friday evening so someone or something else must have happened." Hannah gripped Amy-Rose's hand.

"I suppose I could write a character letter but I shouldn't get involved." Mr Brown's tone was dismissive.

"Because of your desire to be state Governor, do you mean?" Hannah became angry.

"Well yes, partly."

"So it won't go down well with your cohorts if rumours spread that you allow contraband to arrive in the port and you do nothing about it?" Hannah stood, "Amy-Rose go and get your things you're coming home with me."

The girl said nothing as she left the room.

"Are you threatening me, Mrs Phelan?"

"No, I'm not but you see how gossip gathers momentum," Hannah said. "I'll bid you good evening, sir, you can explain to your wife why my daughter has left her service. I assume you'll be good enough to forward any wages due."

"Look, let's not be hasty. Your daughter doesn't need to leave my employ. The two are not linked." Mr Brown sat down again.

"Oh I think they are. She's not safe here. You employed a man who tried to ruin my reputation and attacked my daughter. I'm sure you must have heard rumours about the man, Samuel Fletcher, but chose to ignore them." Hannah stopped talking, her anger spent.

They were not too keen to let her visit Daniel the following morning but relented when she explained the need to dress his wound. He looked dishevelled, dark shadows under his eyes as though he'd had no sleep.

"Tell me what happened again. You know, the truth, what we said, Daniel, come on." Hannah tried to encourage him.

After Daniel had finished speaking, Hannah asked, "I need the names of everyone who was in the hotel with you. Who was Samuel Fletcher talking to?"

"What are you going to do?" he asked.

"I'm going to prove you are innocent, whatever it takes."

"I'll be up before the judge by the end of the week," he stated flatly.

"All the more reason to keep your story straight." She hugged him before leaving him to return to the shop where she asked Amy-Rose to open up while she went first to the doctor's and then to the hotel to talk to anyone who could help.

Hannah spent her evenings copying out the conversations she had, but missed Mary or even Maggie to discuss things with as they had now moved into their new home. She didn't want Amy-Rose in court so took her statement with her on Friday morning.

Daniel was led into the dock looking like a vagabond, a traveller, a miscreant with his hair greasy and matted. He desperately needed a shave. At least the wound down his jawline had scabbed over but it gave his face a sneer. He shuffled to his feet as the judge made his entrance.

Hannah's hands were damp with nerves as she looked at the baying crowd who seemed to be here on a day out. They already seemed to be in agreement that Daniel was guilty. The judge called the crowd to order before asking Daniel how he pleaded on the murder of Samuel Fletcher.

"Not guilty."

Hannah kept her head down. At least Daniel hadn't given up on her. Had she looked to the crowd, she would have seen Gabriel Brown take a seat at the back. The crowd erupted noisily but banging the gavel the judge ordered the prosecution to make their case.

It seemed to take an age for the prosecutor to get to the point but she was determined to have her say otherwise it seemed certain Daniel would go to the gallows. There was a silence as the prosecutor finished, then the judge asked, "Would anyone speak for the defence?"

"I would." Hannah stood to loud guffaws at the thought of a woman speaking in the courtroom and not in the dock.

Hannah began by saying that Daniel, Mr Jerrold, didn't deny that he had fought, though it was little more than a skirmish, with Mr Fletcher on the Friday evening. Both had been drinking, Mr Fletcher had been quite drunk and abusive. She passed the hotel girl's witness statements to the judge.

"To be fair, madam, most men are quite bawdy when alcohol is involved," the judge said as the mob laughed.

"I've never been in a public bar but it can't be right to slander a young girl in that way. What right does anyone have to talk like that with no right of reply? Mr Jerrold didn't like his tone and said so before heading home, however there was an altercation outside the hotel, ending when he was wounded with a horse pick." Hannah passed Amy-Rose's statement to the judge as she held the crowd, getting into her stride. She paused to allow the judge to peruse the single piece of paper before going on. "I would prefer it if the information in the statement remained private, your Honour."

It was quiet now.

"Someone or something must have happened as Mr Fletcher was making his way home," Hannah continued. "I have a doctor's report here which states Mr Fletcher's death was due to being dragged along, probably by the horse and cart. There was bruising on his body from the horses' hooves. The doctor agrees that the loss of blood was too much for his body to cope with. After all, it was several hours before he was found and two days before he passed away."

She passed over the doctor's letter confirming what she had said.

Everyone was listening.

"I would like to call to the stand the gentleman who was with Mr Fletcher when he took his final breath. He is an employee of Mr Gabriel Brown." Hannah was working the crowd and seemed to be quite enjoying her time in the spotlight as her confidence grew.

Whispers went round before a young man stepped in front of the judge.

"Can you tell the court exactly what Mr Fletcher said before he died?" Hannah asked.

"He just said Daniel Jerrold."

"Is that all? He didn't say Daniel Jerrold has killed me?"

"No, no," the boy stammered.

"So he could have been trying to apologise to Mr Jerrold for fighting?" Hannah said loudly, turning to the judge.

"Well suppose."

"Or he could have been trying to say Mr Jerrold was not, I repeat, not, involved." Hannah looked directly at the boy now who turned red.

He didn't answer. Even if he had, it wouldn't have been heard as the court erupted, even the banging of the gavel was drowned out by the shouting. Eventually as the mob calmed down, the judge asked, "Do you have any more to say?"

"No, sir, I do not but I will pass the remaining testimonies to you before you go to reach your decision." Hannah walked over to the judge to pass the remaining statements to him.

"Court adjourned!" The judge stood as did everyone else but Hannah wasn't sure what to do with herself now. She watched Daniel being led back to the cells, the crowd dispersed but she remained motionless. It was over, she had done her best but was it enough, she worried.

It seemed no time at all before the court room started filling up with people again, pushing to get to the front, all standing while the judge bustled back onto the dais.

Hannah looked straight at Daniel, trying to smile, but she was so nervous she couldn't actually get her body to do anything.

Daniel was told to rise as the judge put the black cloth on his head, before saying, "Not guilty. The prisoner is free to go."

Hannah was swept up with the crowd, people she didn't know shaking her hand or patting her unceremoniously on the back as she waited for the rope to be removed from Daniel's wrists.

She watched as he shuffled toward her. She didn't know how she was going to get him home but at least he would be coming home, he was free.

The crowd clapped, and as she helped him down the step, a cart pulled up. Hannah was relieved to see it was Mr Brown who indicated they should climb on board which was difficult so he jumped down to help them both up.

"You never fail to amaze me, Mrs Phelan," Mr Brown stated. "Have you ever thought of becoming a lawyer?"

"I couldn't stand the strain," Hannah replied, looking to Daniel who seemed to have aged in the last few weeks.

The cart stopped outside the shop as Amy-Rose rushed out to help get Daniel inside but she didn't speak to Mr Brown. It was Hannah who said she was grateful for his support.

Hannah didn't really know what to do or say to help Daniel who sat at the table looking at his hands. Pouring water into a bowl, she passed it to him but it wasn't until he'd washed his hands and face that he spoke. "I'm really grateful for your support, Hannah. I don't know what to say to show my gratitude."

Hannah took his hands in hers. "It's over now," but she had realised he was a weak man, she had seen him in a different light over the last few weeks but what could she say? He no longer seemed like the saviour she thought he was. She felt she would never care for him in the same way again.

CHAPTER EIGHTEEN

LIFE'S WHAT YOU MAKE IT

Hannah was unsettled over the next few weeks. There had been so many people coming into the shop to congratulate her. Some had asked if she would represent them in disputes which made her laugh. She didn't ask what the disputes were over or even what she could do to help, what would be the point? As a woman, she had got away with it once but she was sure it wouldn't be condoned by the men in the town on a regular basis.

Her notoriety had even got her name in the town's newspaper much to the embarrassment of the children but she kept it to send to Dan when she next wrote a letter.

Her business was booming but she was struggling to keep up with demand. She was even beginning to wish she had taken up the awful Captain Munroe's offer. Hannah really felt the need to do something different but wasn't sure what. After her experience in the courtroom there was the need to stretch her brain more.

She was also unsettled that her relationship with Daniel was at odds, though neither had actually spoken about it. To her mind, he seemed to have been in a rush to return to his flat and work as though he was on fire. Hannah had offered to give up her bed so she could care for him until he was well but he refused, even though she thought it was too soon for him to be on his own. They had been in each other's company only once since he had been released when he seemed angry, brooding somehow, but she didn't ask why.

It was difficult to talk at Dennis and Mary's where free-range children were running around having fun on Sundays when they all descended for a picnic. To Hannah's mind, he had tried not be left alone with her and it hurt, but she couldn't, wouldn't ask him what was wrong between them.

The weeks turned into months, then a new year and people stopped asking when they were going to marry because they didn't want the backlash from Hannah. She had stopped sending him an evening meal and he refrained from going over to Mary's so their paths didn't cross.

She stopped going over and over their last conversations, deciding she was better on her own to care for the children. The sticking point was the house and land that was part-owned with Daniel, as was the small house next door, though this was now rented out but she took no income from it, after all it was his money that had paid for it.

In her mind she wondered how she could have got herself in this mess again, first with Adam and now Daniel. She still paid rent to Maggie for her house, and it all sounded so complicated but it suited Hannah to remain where she was. She had the small bedroom while the three girls shared, although one set of bunk beds had now gone to Mary and her ever increasing family.

There had been persistent drizzle over the last few days that seeped into everything and Hannah hadn't been over the doorstep. Kitty and Victoria took themselves off to school while Amy-Rose helped in the shop when asked but she really needed to find another job. Hannah regretted taking her from the Browns and the money would certainly have come in handy.

She didn't get many customers when the weather was inclement so she was surprised to see Mary so early in the morning with Rory sitting in the perambulator.

"Right, Amy-Rose, will you entertain his highness while I talk to your mam?" Mary pushed the baby toward her.

"Hello, what brings you out on a day like this, as if I didn't know?" Hannah hugged her friend who was now pregnant with her fourth child.

"I want to know what's going on with you and Daniel? I know I've asked before and you've never given me an answer, so come on spit it out." Mary sat herself on the couch.

"I'll give you the same answer, I don't know. Things have never been right since he was in court and I haven't seen him in months." Hannah spoke sadly.

"Dennis said he's miserable, hardly speaks, just grunts, and snaps at the two young men."

"What do you expect me to do about it? He knows where I am," Hannah said, exasperated.

"Be the bigger person, Hannah, and go and talk to him for goodness sake and find out what's wrong with him. If it's over then at least you can move on," Mary told her.

"Move on? I don't think I want anyone in my life. My girls are enough for me," she replied, wondering if that were really true.

"If you don't want to marry him then release him from your promise. After all, you are the real reason he came to Australia. I won't stop nagging until you sort this out." Mary struggled to get up again.

"I'll think about it. Will that do?" Hannah hugged Mary again.

"Make sure you do, now I must be off before Corrine drives Maggie to despair. She's into everything these days. Corrine, not Maggie."

They both laughed before Hannah said, "Oh, I do miss you, you know."

"Well, move in next door. It's almost ready."

"Look, I'm not going into that now. It's just so much easier to live in the shop. Now get away with you." Hannah opened the door.

After they had waved Mary off, Amy-Rose said, "You know she's right. None of us know what's going on."

"I'm sorry, I didn't realise. As I said, let me think about it. Now will you take that letter to the post office to send to Dan." Hannah needed a few minutes to herself. She hadn't realised how being inert had affected so many people, making the decision to go and talk to

Daniel the following Saturday. The girls would be fine for an hour. She was apprehensive about the reception she would receive but knew something would have to be done.

She was ready to shut the shop when the bell rang, bringing in Mr Brown who she hadn't seen since he dropped her and Daniel off from the court.

"Mrs Phelan, I hope I find you well?"

"Yes, thank you and yourself?"

"Never better, never better. Now I'll come straight to the point if I may? I have a proposition, well two actually, to put to you if you can spare a few minutes?"

"I'm intrigued, Mr Brown."

"The first is to do with Amy-Rose. Is she here?"

Hannah called her daughter, through from the kitchen. Amy-Rose seemed embarrassed to see Mr Brown again.

"My two boys will be going to school in England next year but their education still needs a little, more than a little, in English and Mathematics. Their tutor has given them a good grounding in Latin, History and the Classics, so here's what I have in mind if you would consider returning to my employ?"

Hannah looked to Amy-Rose who agreed readily before she even knew what he was proposing.

"If you would return as before, the morning you would spend with the boys and the afternoon with my wife, who still hasn't forgiven me for your leaving so you'd be doing me a great favour," he smiled, lighting up his whole face.

"What do you think?" Hannah looked at her daughter.

"Of course your wage would increase to six shilling in line with the fact you will be teaching and you would live in during the week as before."

"And what was your other proposition?" Hannah asked.

"You are aware I am running for Town Mayor?"

"Yes, what's that got to do with Amy-Rose?"

"I'd like you to come and talk at the Town Hall as part of my campaign."

"Me, why me? Oh, I don't think so," Hannah said, shocked at the thought of standing up in front of people.

"You captivated the crowd at the court, they listened to you and as a business woman you could explain about the opportunities here for everyone. What do you say?"

"As a woman I don't even get a vote so I don't think I'd be much help. If I marry, my property then belongs to my husband and I have to give up employment so I don't think I can help, sorry." Hannah knew she could have gone on about the inequalities of being a woman.

"Yes, yes, I agree but you have managed to remove the shackles by being successful, making your way in this country. Look, don't make a decision now, think about it, will you?" Mr Brown held out his hand. "I'll call again on Monday for both your decisions if I may?"

The thoughts of Daniel were forgotten as Hannah and Amy-Rose talked at length about both opportunities. For Amy-Rose, it would be the opportunity of a lifetime even though the post would only be for twelve months until Mr Brown's boys left for school. Hannah wasn't so sure about her offer but agreed with her children that she wouldn't make a hasty decision one way or the other.

They all went to church the following morning before going for lunch at Mary's where there was plenty to talk about and as usual Mary was the voice of reason.

"You have to do it, Hannah, you have to stand up for women everywhere."

"Perhaps you should do it, you seem to have plenty to say on the matter," Hannah replied.

Everyone seemed to be in agreement. It would be a wonderful opportunity for her to have a voice. So on the following Monday when Mr Brown arrived, Amy-Rose was ready to return to the house and Hannah agreed to speak.

"You can read what I am going to say but I don't want you to amend the content or sentiment," Hannah told him defiantly.

"No, I don't expect to but it will help with my speech if I can read it."

Hannah paced around the kitchen, chewing the end of her pencil, reading, writing, amending. Looking at her hands, they looked like an old lady's, wrinkled and worn. They were working hands from being a child collecting eggs or hoeing the vegetable plot. When she first married, she scrubbed, cleaned, washed until her fingers were numb before ending up at the correction facility here in Cheapside where she untangled lambswool, her hands red raw and sore. Her nails were short, snagged, but it gave her an idea what she could write about.

So for the next week or so Hannah wrote and rewrote her speech before reading it aloud to herself, amending any words she tripped over. Her first test was to read it to Kitty and Victoria who clapped loudly when she finished. Amy-Rose suggested one or two changes but it was Mary who was her severest critic, but even she agreed it was good.

The nerves were starting to jangle as people began taking their seats in the main room of the Town Hall. They came in dribs and drabs before the whole room seemed to fill quickly. Hannah spotted her family sitting with Mary and Dennis, surprised to see Daniel sitting with them.

Mr Brown sat next to her, talking amicably with his opponents, but she sat trying not to get eye contact with anyone.

Listening to the first man explain his reasons for wanting to be the next Mayor, Hannah thought he had some good ideas and if she had a vote he would have got it, but then so would the next man. Then suddenly Mr Brown began his speech and then it was her turn. There was silence in the room. She felt everyone's eyes on her, faltering she began by holding up her hands.

"These hands, my hands have toiled in the earth to provide food for the table. Using these hands I have helped family and friends build a home, a life in this young country. When we arrived here, this was a backwater or empty quarter as it was known but look at what we have today. We have seen the arrival of men with skills to build the railway as well as those who will use their strength to dig out the new harbour. None of this would be possible without our hands."

She looked around and continued. "Look at Mrs Coyle who runs the post office, Mrs Jobson who keeps everyone in line at the hotel. I run my own business. Women's hands may be more gentle, cooking, sewing, cleaning or tucking our children into bed but is our work less important? What kind of legacy do we leave our children? Mother's, wives forgotten. We can build a country to be proud of if we all hold each other's hands but we need to step out of the shadows, celebrate the good things, seek to achieve the best we can for everyone. Thank you for listening." Hannah looked at Mr Brown before returning to her seat.

He continued with his address, agreeing with Hannah about working together. He finished by thanking Hannah. Once the applause was over, those on the stage mingled with the crowd. Hannah spoke to a number of people before making her way to her friends. She was embarrassed when Daniel spoke to her.

Deciding she had to do something, Hannah said, "We need to talk, Daniel. Would you like to come for a meal one night next week?"

He mumbled something that she didn't catch but she continued, "Pick a night. The girls will be pleased to see you."

They agreed on the Thursday with Mary whispering that she would call in on the Friday for the details, before Hannah was called away to have her photograph taken with Mr and Mrs Brown. By the time she returned to her friends, Daniel had left, which infuriated her. What was wrong with him?

Amy-Rose returned to the Browns while Hannah and the girls walked part way back with Mary and Dennis. All the talk was about the evening, what it would mean for the town and more importantly who would win the upcoming election, though Hannah was preoccupied with what was wrong with Daniel.

On the Thursday evening, he arrived looking smart, his hair washed and he had shaved, the scar on his jaw lighter now but still visible. The conversation was difficult, no that's not true, the conversation with Hannah was difficult, and most of the talk went through the girls who were happy to tell him what they had been doing. It was only after they finished the meal that Hannah asked Kitty and Victoria to wash up while she picked up the two mugs of tea and she motioned for Daniel to follow her into the shop.

Hannah spoke immediately before her confidence left her. "What's going on Daniel, with us, I mean?"

Looking at her forlornly. he replied, "You've got your life and I've got mine."

"What does that mean?"

"I don't feel comfortable mixing in your circle of friends like the Browns. I don't have the conversation or education to compete. You are much cleverer than me, you with your fancy words and reading. You're so comfortable mixing with everyone. I'm not sociable like you. I'd just hold you back. I'm happy on my own and I can't give you what you want, Hannah."

"You don't know what I want because you've never asked me and I wouldn't call the Browns friends."

"Well, you certainly seem to spend a lot of time cosying up to him."

"What on earth are you talking about? I'm trying to make a life here for my family so what do you expect me to do? Sit at home sewing?" Hannah became annoyed.

"You've made a good life here and you don't need me for that. I'll always be your friend and care for you, Hannah."

"Care for me? Well that's alright then."

"Don't be like that, Hannah. That's what I mean. I'm no good with words. If you want me to say I love you, I will."

"It doesn't mean anything if you have to be told. Don't say any more, just don't. If that's how you feel, I thought you loved me but caring isn't enough for either of us, we need to sort things out as amicably as possible." She paused to gather her thoughts, trying not to let her emotions get the better of her. "I'd like to sell my share of the house and take my name off the place next door. It's not mine," Hannah said, hoping for a response.

"If that's what you want." Daniel stood up. "I'll sort it out." With that, he opened the shop door stepping out into the night and Hannah's life.

CHAPTER NINETEEN
TWISTS AND TURNS

Hannah sat for a long time wondering what had just happened. He would always care for her? That's what he said. What was she supposed to say to that? That's it, then, it's over. Daniel didn't want to be with her after all they had been through. She always thought they would grow old together, that it was just a matter of timing and perhaps that was it. She hadn't rushed into marrying him and they had taken each other for granted for so long. What was she going to tell the girls and more to the point what was she going to say to Mary?

She thought she would have begged him, thought she would cry but had done neither. Instead, strangely it was somehow relief. He could get on with his life and more importantly so could she instead of having the dark cloud hanging over her. It wasn't what she thought would happen but in the same breath she wasn't disappointed.

Hugging Kitty and Victoria to her, she explained she wasn't sad and they could all now move on. It would be more difficult to explain to Amy-Rose and Mary.

The year 1885 passed with Mary having another daughter, Belle, on the third of May, while Hannah was busy trying to make ends meet.

Daniel had been quick in sending her two solicitors' letters. The first straightforward, the property next door, all she needed to do was sign the letter and return. The second was a little more complicated. It was an offer to purchase the land for what monies she had put into it. Hannah was sure it would be worth more now it had a house on it but had no indication as to what that value would be. She really didn't want to go and talk to Daniel and a solicitor would cost money. Perhaps Dennis would have some idea of what their house was now worth.

It was Mr Brown who came to her aid, showing her a piece in the newspaper stating land prices had increased around 11% and this is what she should be asking for, however if the case took months to agree it could be worth a bit more. Hannah calculated she could be due almost £50, a lot of money for her, so drafted a letter in reply taking it to the solicitors' office herself.

She was happy not to claim anything for the house as Daniel had paid for all the wood as well as his time building it, a house she would no longer live in. Both her and Mary were disappointed they would not be neighbours but that was unavoidable.

A further letter arrived with an increased offer so Hannah accepted, going to the solicitors to collect a cheque. Before taking it to the only bank in town to cash it, she called into the post office to see if she had any post. She hadn't but Mrs Coyle did inform Hannah that they were selling the property to move the business to a larger place closer to the timber yard. She would also be selling the goodwill of the post office and haberdashery.

Hannah was intrigued but said nothing immediately. She was sure she would need to borrow money if she decided to buy it.

Within twelve months Hannah had purchased the post office building with the help of a bank loan, countersigned by Mr Brown as well as moving into the flat above. She designed a new interior downstairs leaving the post office counter where it was but making the haberdashery smaller, taking the bookcases from the shop.

Dennis built a partition wall to separate the hardware side with a door to allow them access to the stairs and kitchen. Everything seemed different but for the first time in years Hannah felt settled. This was her home, no rent to pay on it only the loan, but one day she would own the building outright and when she had enough money she had an idea for the empty space.

Hannah thought her life was settled. Amy-Rose was almost seventeen and her time teaching Mr Brown's sons would soon be over but she had agreed to stay on full time with Mrs Brown. She told Hannah the whole household was strained with the boys going and one of the nannies going back to look after them in the school holidays at the family home.

When she was home at the weekend, she was happy to learn about the post office as was Kitty who would leave school next year still determined to train as a teacher. Victoria at twelve had her mother, Lizzie's, temperament, being very easy going and a happy young lady.

Hannah hadn't given up the second hand goods completely but didn't go out to auctions anymore, she was busy enough with the post office and shop, though people did come in with things occasionally, which she still bought to put on the shelves.

The new year of 1887 brought a number of changes for Hannah and her family. Mary had her fifth child, a boy Seamus, on the second of February, her house always overflowing and noisy.

Dan was now twenty-three and still not much of a writer so she was surprised when a letter arrived from America in a handwriting she didn't recognise.

Fearing the worst, she opened it to see a photograph of her son looking so handsome in his uniform, his tricorn hat under his arm, but what surprised her more was the woman sitting in the chair next to him. His arm was on her shoulder but not only did she look much older than Dan but she was rather plain, old fashioned judging by the clothing and the white lace toque on her head. She looked like a woman rather than a girl.

The letter was written by the woman in the photograph, Matilda Abraham, who was now engaged to Hannah's son. Her words were pleasant, friendly and interesting, explaining about her family in America and how they had met. They were to marry in two years' time when Dan finished his training before moving into a home that had been left to her by her paternal grandmother.

What surprised Hannah even more was that two tea chests had been sent to her with items from the grandmother's as Dan had explained she had a shop selling second hand goods. She was intrigued as to what could possibly be in them and when they would arrive, promising herself to reply as soon as they did.

Weeks later when the two chests arrived it was like Christmas for the whole family. They unpacked them carefully when they realised most of it was china. There were a number of tea sets with matching tea pots wrapped tightly in linen tablecloths and napkins. The sugar bowls and milk jugs were as delicate as the rest of the crockery.

The idea which had been in Hannah's mind for some time seemed to be finally coming to fruition but first she had to clean and decorate the old hardware part of the shop that was now a dumping ground.

Hannah waited until the Saturday when Amy-Rose could look after the shop while Hannah and the girls set to sweeping, washing and generally clearing out the room. Hannah intended painting the walls with distemper to freshen the place up while Kitty and Victoria did their homework and prepare the vegetables for tea. It took her a long time with paint dripping on her hands and face so she was embarrassed when Amy-Rose popped her head through the door to say Mr Brown would like a word.

She attempted to wipe her face with her hand but it made it worse so she no longer had spots of white paint but war stripes across her cheeks.

Mr Brown laughed when he saw her. "Oh, you look busy. I thought your friends helped with this kind of thing?" He swept his arm wide.

"Be careful, don't get paint on your jacket. Dennis has enough to do with his ever growing family, five they have now, though this may have been more relaxing for him."

"What about Mr Jerrold? I thought he was a close friend?"

"Not anymore. He has his life and I have mine," Hannah said sadly.

"I'm sorry, I didn't mean to pry or embarrass you."

"No, it's fine, water under the bridge and all that. Anyway, you haven't come here to discuss my social life so what can I do for you?" Hannah said.

"We are opening a Literary Institute in the new Town Hall and I would like to invite you," Mr Brown said.

"I'm really busy at the moment so it would be difficult." Hannah really didn't want to go.

"Well, you don't know when it is yet, it's not for a few weeks and it's an evening, the sixth of November, so you have plenty of time to get organised.

"That's my birthday," Hannah said almost to herself.

"All the more reason to do something. Mrs Brown will be attending and we can collect you on the way," he said, trying to back her into a corner.

"You are persistent."

"What? Like a fly buzzing around that you'd like to swat," Mr Brown grinned and Hannah couldn't help but to join in. "Unless you have another appointment, I won't take no for an answer."

"Let me think about it and I'll let you know. Will that do?" Hannah told him. "Now I'm sorry, I must get on."

After weeks of getting everything ready, Hannah had managed to purchase chairs from the old Town Hall and the tables had been made for her by the carpenter. The sign writer had made a new sign that Hannah had designed herself. All the baking had been done, the butcher and baker delivered their goods and everything was ready to go.

At nine o'clock on a Monday morning, the Primrose Tea Room was opened with no fanfare. The sign showed the proprietor as Hannah Phelan and daughters. For a set price, to be paid at the post office counter, people could come in to socialise over tea, sandwiches and cake. It seemed a little decadent but Hannah knew there was nowhere in the town for ladies to meet, though it was open to all.

It started off slowly. Amy-Rose was now working in the post

office full time, and that allowed Hannah to concentrate on the tea room. She had made sure everything was ready, trays set up in the kitchen, water boiling and tea pots, spouts all facing the same way like soldiers on parade. She wished she had kept in touch with James and Primmy who would be overwhelmed that the place was named after her.

People arrived slowly, not quite sure what to do, but by lunch time she was full, rushing backward and forward, clearing tables as quickly as she could. By the time Kitty and Victoria returned from school, Hannah was exhausted, sitting for a few moments while they did the clearing and washing up, carefully, she kept telling them.

By the time her birthday came round, the last thing she wanted to do was go out and socialise but Mr Brown would be collecting her in the next half hour. Hannah changed into her best dress while Victoria did her hair so she was standing in the shop waiting when the trap arrived.

Mr Brown was alone, much to Hannah's dismay. His wife was indisposed, he told her. The stress of going back to England in the next week had given her a headache. She was returning to their home to be close to the boys and would not be returning. Hannah was embarrassed to arrive with Mr Brown, especially when he put his hand on her elbow to help her up the step. To her surprise, the evening went better than she thought as she managed to promote her new business venture to the ladies who promised to call in.

Those who came into the post office to collect parcels or letters now stayed for a chat. Even Mrs Coyle and Mrs Jobson called to see what it was all about. It had become so busy Hannah had taken on a girl from Kitty's class who had already left school. She hoped to train her as a waitress but at present she was confined to the kitchen doing more of the menial tasks.

Two weeks before Christmas and Hannah was almost on her knees but grateful that the girls would soon finish school for the holidays so could help out though she decided to close between

Christmas and New Year because people wouldn't have much money to spend rather spending time with their families.

The girls were in their room as she sat at the kitchen table counting out the day's takings when there was a knock on the back door, making her jump. Throwing a tea towel over the money before opening the door, she saw Daniel standing looking sheepish. She was surprised, shocked even, to see him after all this time but welcomed him in. The conversation was a little stilted at first as he asked about the girls, though Hannah had an idea why he was here. Mary had already told her that he had been invited to theirs for dinner on Christmas day but she waited for him to say it.

However before he managed to spit anything out, there was a loud rap on the shop door. Excusing herself she picked up the keys to open the door where she found Mr Brown in a state.

"What's wrong, what's happened?" Hannah asked concerned.

"Terrible news, terrible news," Mr Brown sobbed.

Hannah had no option but to invite him in.

"Look, sit here and I'll get you a drink." She pulled out a chair. This was going to be embarrassing but when she went through to the kitchen, Daniel was gone.

Closing and locking the back door before pouring out another cup of tea, she placed Daniel's cup into the sink. Hannah returned to Mr Brown who was drying his eyes with a handkerchief.

"What on earth has happened to get you in such a state?"

"My wife and girls are dead, drowned." He couldn't say more.

"Oh, I'm so sorry to hear that but how do you know?" Hannah asked putting her hand over his for comfort.

"The captain of the ship which docked today came to see me, told me there had been a terrible storm off the Cape of Good Hope. Several ships were lost, including the one my family were on."

"I'm so sorry." Hannah couldn't think of anything else to say.

"It's my fault. She never wanted to come here in the first place and now they are dead." He wiped his eyes again.

"You can't be blamed. It's God's will. He chooses when we live or die. What about the boys? Who will tell them? Will you go home now?" Hannah knew she was gabbling but didn't know how to deal with his angst.

"No, I need to stay here for my work. The boys will go to her parents for the holidays. Look, I'm sorry I've bothered you but I had to talk to someone."

"I'm glad you felt you could come to me, now how about sharing some supper, only what's left from today. I wish I had something stronger to offer you but I've only tea, I'm afraid."

Hannah went into the kitchen as Mr Brown followed her, watching as she put out clean plates and cups.

"Oh look, I'm stopping you." He looked at the paper and money on the table.

"It's not a problem, it won't take long. I was just cashing up and I like to keep the businesses separate so I can keep track of the profits."

They talked for a little while longer but Hannah stiffened slightly when he hugged her as he thanked her for listening.

"Will you be alright, you know, getting home?" she asked for something to say.

"I've left the horse at the stables and he knows the way and I'll have a few strong ones when I get to my bed."

Hannah watched him walk toward the hotel, wondering what Daniel would make of that, would he be jealous or had that boat sailed? More to the point, she felt sad to think that in a house full of people, Mr Brown had no one he could talk to. Should she have invited him to Mary's, they wouldn't mind another mouth to feed, but perhaps not, the house would be pandemonium with children everywhere.

Hannah was surprised on Christmas Eve when one of the butlers from the Browns came with a handwritten invitation for everyone to go to the big house for a New Year's Eve party. There would be staff on hand in the nursery for Mary's children and he had invited Daniel and anyone else she could think of.

When she took the invite to show Mary, she was adamant that they would go, after all she had never had the opportunity to look around the place and this was probably her only opportunity. Even Maggie was keen to put on her best and mix with whoever else was there so it was agreed. The only one to turn down the offer was Daniel who had arrived at Mary's with his new friend Jeannie, who had worked in the laundry with Mary years ago. Daniel was embarrassed but Hannah was relieved and the woman seemed nice enough though a little sheepish and mousy but perhaps she was being just a touch jealous.

Once all the celebrations were over and life returned to some kind of normality Hannah took stock of how far she had come. Never in a million years would she have had two businesses in England or where for the first time in her life money wasn't a problem. Once the bank loan was paid off she would own this property herself. Yes, Mr Brown had countersigned for the loan but it would be hers soon.

Hannah became worried when she hadn't seen Mr Brown for some months after the New Year's Eve party. The house was full to bursting with copious amounts of food and drink consumed well into the night. Everyone seemed to be having a good time and she hadn't been able to speak to him about how he was coping. She'd had to stop Mary and Maggie doing a tour around the place but they all agreed as they carried tired children home that it had been the best New Year ever.

Days went into weeks, then months and Hannah was beginning to worry about Mr Brown. She could see how busy he was at work with all the digging out of the river channel to expand the dock area. The whole place would change the face of the town forever and there would be plenty of work for all who wanted it, that was the promise. Hannah hoped that was true as she still saw children in ragged clothes and no shoes, hanging around looking for scraps or pennies.

CHAPTER TWENTY

ARE WE FRIENDS?

She decided she would have to go up to the house herself to ask about Mr Brown's well being. He thought of her as a friend after all, so what was wrong with that? Once the tea shop had closed for the day, Hannah left the girls with instructions to lock the back door. She would take the shop keys with her. If she was late, she assured them, Mr Brown would provide a trap so not to worry.

Hannah was apprehensive as she walked up the drive, sure one of the staff would have seen her though the place looked deserted with no one in the garden at all. Knocking loudly, Hannah seemed to wait an age so she knocked again but nothing. She wasn't sure what to do. As she had walked all this way and not wanting to waste the journey, she tried the door. It was unlocked. Going inside, she called out but it echoed around the hallway. Standing still, she listened, heard nothing, no steps, no creaking doors, nothing. It was strange and Hannah called again, tapping on the parlour door before looking inside. The curtains were closed making the room gloomy. Moving down the corridor, Hannah tried to remember where Mr Brown's study was. She rapped on the door she thought was the right one before opening it.

Mr Brown was seated, head on the desk with a tumbler and an open bottle of spirit close to his arm. Hannah wasn't sure if he was drunk or asleep so she tried to back out of the room but moved too far to the side, kicking a small table and making Mr Brown raise his head. Hoping he hadn't seen her, she moved to the door but he called, "Mrs Phelan," rubbing his hands over his face.

Walking back into the room, she said as lightly as she could, "Oh there you are, I thought the whole place was empty. How are you? I was worried about you."

He answered, slurring his words so she couldn't make out what he said, so she continued, "Where are the staff? There is no one about." She thought he'd said sacked but couldn't believe that was possible. Surely she would have known. "Stay there and I'll get you something to eat and drink then you need to go to bed to sleep this off."

Opening the door on the opposite side to the parlour, she came to a dining room, though it no longer had furniture in it. Hannah could hear voices coming through the door on the opposite wall. She wasn't sure why but she crossed the room as quietly as she could, flinging the door wide open. She didn't know who was more surprised, her or the staff sitting round the table.

"Who are you?" someone said.

"If you had bothered to answer the door, I would have made myself known. Now could you make up a tray of tea and something light to eat for Mr Brown. Who is his valet?" Hannah looked to the men at the end of the table.

"I am."

"Well, go and draw down his bed covers. Once he's eaten, he will be retiring for the night. Bring the tray through to the study, will you?" Hannah turned to go but heard someone whisper, "Who does she think she is? The lady of the house?"

She turned back angrily. " I don't think I'm anyone but myself so I suggest you get on with your work."

She was smiling as she returned to the study to see Mr Brown had gone back to sleep. Taking the bottle and glass, she placed them on a side table, before opening the curtains, bringing in the early evening light.

"Mr Brown, wake up," she said gently. "Mr Brown." His head moved, only sitting up when the maid came in with the tray. "Come on now, get something into you then you can sleep." She dismissed the girl and poured out the tea, putting plenty of milk and sugar in it.

Pushing his head up so it propped itself on the back of the chair, she tried to get him to sip but he groaned, dribbling the tea down his chin. This was no good, he needed to go to bed to sleep it off. Putting her arm on his back, Hannah tried to get him up but he was a dead weight.

Returning to the kitchen, she knew what kind of reception she would get but didn't care. The staff were pretending to look busy but she asked two of the men to go with her to help Mr Brown to his room.

She didn't go up the stairs with them. "I want you to make sure he has something to eat when he wakes. Is that clear?" And with that she made her way back down the drive and home.

All she could think of was that poor man on his own. You never imagine anyone with so many people around to be lonely. Where were his supposed friends? Those happy to take his hospitality. She was one of them but that would all change.

The following day being Sunday she met Mary at church before walking back to hers for lunch. She explained what had happened and how the staff had been sat idle.

"Do you want me to come with you to see if he's alright?" Mary asked.

"No, but if you don't mind I'll slip along after lunch. The girls can help with the clearing and washing up and I can pick them up on my way back."

She knew she wouldn't be popular with the staff but was surprised when she knocked on the door and it was opened almost immediately.

"Where's Mr Brown?" she asked, going into the hall uninvited.

"In his study, shall I tell him you're here?"

"Yes, please do."

Mr Brown strode down the hallway looking much better than yesterday though he still had dark circles under his eyes. "Mrs Phelan, I apologise most sincerely for my demeanour yesterday. It had been a trying day at work and… well, anyway."

"I hope you feel a little better today. I should have called sooner to see how you were coping."

"The staff said you gave them a kick up their backside, not their words exactly but I got the gist."

"They were sitting round doing nothing. It seemed they had left you to the mercy of the bottle so I said a few things but nothing much." She tried not to laugh. "Well, if you are going to leave me standing here, I'll get myself away."

"I'm sorry, where are my manners? Come into the parlour. There's a couple of comfy seats there."

Hannah looked at the room. She hadn't noticed before but many of the pictures and ornaments were gone.

As if reading her mind, he said, "They were packed up to go back to England. Old Neptune's got them now."

"Oh I'm sorry."

"Let's call a truce and both stop apologising. Would you like tea?" he grinned.

"Yes, that would be nice." Hannah sat, not really knowing what else to say.

"You know, the staff don't have enough to do. I've cut down but some of them came over with us."

"Well, would any of them return if you arranged it?"

"I don't know."

"Perhaps you should get them together and ask. That would be a start."

"Straight away ma'am." He stood to attention, making them both laugh loudly.

"I could do with a waitress but they wouldn't be able to live in," Hannah said, "but I could cover their wages."

"One down only ninety nine to go." Mr Brown smiled.

"You haven't got a hundred staff. Have you?"

"I have no idea how many. Do you think that's terrible?"

"I do, Mr Brown, you could be taken advantage of."

"Please, Gabriel, surely we know each other well enough now to be on first name terms. Anything else you want to injure me with while I'm down?"

"Oh you." Hannah couldn't help but laugh. "I see you are much improved so I'll be on my way."

"To say thank you for your concern, would you like to have tea with me one day. I hear there is a wonderful tea shop in town."

"That's enough. The drink has addled your brain but you are welcome there anytime." Hannah stepped out of the door. "Goodnight, Gabriel."

"Goodnight, Hannah. May I call you that? Look, wait a minute, I'll walk back with you."

"It's alright, I am only going to Mary's to collect the girls. I'll be fine."

Gabriel Brown watched her walk down the drive and Hannah knew he was watching. She thought about turning to wave but didn't.

All Hannah told Mary was that Mr Brown was now fine. She didn't want to discuss the conversation. She wanted to keep it to herself to mull over.

The following Saturday just as Hannah was closing the tea shop, Gabriel Brown breezed in with a number of books under his arm. "A peace offering."

"Take a seat and join me for a cup of tea." Hannah brought a plate of left over delicacies and sat opposite her friend. That's how it started. He called in once a week with a painting for the wall or more books, anything, and always stayed for a chat.

Mary gave birth to her sixth child on the fourteenth of July 1888, a son Patrick, and declared this was to be her last, with three boys and three girls she had done her bit for the population. It was the family Mary never had. Her father had left her with an alcoholic mother when she was just a toddler and from the age of five she was left to go out stealing to buy food and ale. By the time she met Hannah she had been in gaol numerous times for pickpocketing. She always promised that her children would have a better life in a loving home. Hannah was happy to play auntie to them all. On the other hand, she was glad that her girls were almost grown. Dennis, the proud father, was relieved that their family was now complete.

CHAPTER TWENTY-ONE

THE FINAL CHAPTER

As the last decade of the century breezed in, many things changed in Cheapside and more so for Hannah and her family. She began writing items for a new magazine especially for women, which started in Australia. Kitty was keen to write from a young woman's point of view so were both excited when the editor arranged a visit to the Literary Institute in town.

The editor Louisa Lawson stated that any charge for tickets should be given to widows and the poor of the area instead of paying her a fee. Hannah was pleased to see more women than men, sitting with bated breath, in silence as the woman took to the stage. She was a smart well-dressed young woman wearing a matching jacket and skirt but Hannah was surprised at how young she was.

Miss Lawson looked confidently out on the crowd. "I want to begin with words attributed to William Wilberforce, though I would dispute that, but please bear with me. Ask yourself why we have repressed people, oppressed people, tortured and murdered for the worst possible reasons, the colour of their skin? What has happened is tragic, terrible but we could say the same for women. How many women do you see with black eyes, broken noses, bruising on their bodies. Why?"

It reminded Hannah of the physical and mental torture she suffered in the hands of her first husband and how she would never put up with that again from anyone.

The women were entranced, occasionally nodding, as Miss Lawson talked for over an hour. It impressed Hannah that she managed to talk with no notes, no pauses and no uncomfortable silences.

No one was in a hurry to leave the hall as they vied to get a word with the speaker but there was a crowd around her so Hannah was about to leave with Kitty when Gabriel came over with Louisa Lawson in tow.

After the introductions, they talked for a short while about what Hannah had been up to. Miss Lawson was keen to learn more, inviting Hannah for lunch at the hotel the following day. She was about to decline because of work when Gabriel intervened. "Why don't you go to Hannah's tea shop and see for yourself?"

For the first time since opening, Hannah put a reserved sign on the best table by the window overlooking the street. She was nervous, not sure what she could talk about but was sure Louisa Lawson would have plenty to say.

The outcome of the discussion was an invite for Hannah to travel to Perth to meet other like-minded women. As she had never been out of Cheapside, it worried her. She had never seen any of the country that was now her home. Everyone encouraged her to go, to see what was going on. She could travel by train and stay in a hotel but she worried about going on her own.

Amy-Rose said she could cope with the post office but what surprised Hannah most was Kitty wanted to go with her. She would ask for some time off. Even Victoria joined in, saying she could organise the tea shop.

Before she knew it, here they were at the railway station waiting for the train to arrive, Kitty excited, Hannah apprehensive. They were surprised at the greenery not far out of the town. The railway seemed to cut a swathe through a jungle. Hannah remembered Daniel's anecdotes about strange animals and insects everywhere. He always said if they didn't bite, you they would eat you.

The city itself was much larger and more modern than Cheapside that felt like the poor relation in comparison. Everything from shops to people feeling more confident made the two of them very much like country cousins. If Hannah had been alone, she would never have ventured out from the confines of the hotel but Kitty was keen to explore so they walked through parks, looked at buildings, even taking tea in a different hotel.

The gathering of women opened Hannah's eyes to the things others were doing for their communities and what was missing in hers. She would certainly have plenty to talk about when she returned home. The Women's Movement was gathering pace, pressing for votes both in Australia and England. Hannah signed up to receive the paper, which was written and produced by women, on a regular basis to put in the tea shop for others to read when she finished with it.

She enjoyed the time away with Kitty who turned out to be a confident personable young lady who was happy to talk to everyone. On the return journey they both talked about what they could get involved in and how they could improve the lives of women in the town. They had so many ideas but Hannah realised that in order to put some into action she would need to raise funds from the very people who were against many of the policies, but that didn't put her off.

They were woken early one morning to a cacophony of shouting, feet running and horses' hooves going up and down the street at a gallop. Hannah went out to see what was going on to be told the dam had breached, causing flooding and mayhem with injured, dying men everywhere.

The Phelan women set to in an attempt to help. Victoria ran to the doctor's surgery to see what help was needed, while Amy-Rose boiled water. Kitty and Hannah put chairs out on the street for the injured to sit. Victoria returned with a box of bandages, iodine as well as a needle and thread, setting to helping those with minor wounds. The horses and carts were taking the severely injured onto one of the ships for treatment as there was no hospital in town.

Amy-Rose was sent to the hardware store for tin mugs while

Hannah and Kitty made sandwiches before Victoria asked for help to clean and bandage the wounds. The girl didn't flinch, even when the men did, but sewed up eyebrows, hands, legs with a neatness good enough for dressmaking. Hannah held the man with a dislocated collarbone as Victoria put her slight weight behind it until she heard the loud crack and it was done.

They made tea, tea and more tea throughout the day, putting in plenty of sugar for the shock and nerves but it was early afternoon before she spotted Gabriel half carrying a man who was struggling to stand upright. Going to meet them, Hannah grabbed the other arm and got him to a chair before taking Gabriel inside. She gave him a drink and a sandwich, asking, "What happened?"

"The spring tide, it was higher than normal. It breached the top of the dam It was too strong. The men tried to put stays against the beams to shore it up but it didn't hold. Those closest to it have drowned. They didn't stand a chance. What a mess!"

"You won't be able to do anything until low tide so let's just concentrate on what we can do. Do you think your cook could make a pan of soup or something? Everyone needs to be fed. That would be a start. We'll carry on here."

The flow of men drifting up from the docks dwindled to an odd one or two and Hannah assumed that the worst was over. Those still sitting on the chairs had been treated expertly by Victoria who hadn't stopped but she was in her element. Hannah watched as she took control as though she had been doing it for years with such an easy manner with all the men.

Eventually a cart arrived with a huge pan of soup. Hannah and Amy-Rose struggled to carry it into the kitchen so they decanted it into smaller pans, warming it up, and the baker brought bread which was broken into small shives.

By the end of the day, the four women were exhausted, slowly carrying chairs back into the shop, the walking wounded now gone home. Victoria said she would go to the ship the following day to see if she could be any help.

The whole town was shocked to an eerie silence at what had happened, none more so than Gabriel Brown, who felt it was his fault it happened. He told Hannah that he had miscalculated the amount of water hitting the dam and they would have to shore it up before work could start again which could take months.

Although she had sympathy for him and those who had lost their lives, she knew they had to help those who were injured, widowed and out of work.

"Do you think your cook could make a pan of soup each day to feed those families affected? I would be able to serve it from the shop," she asked.

"I don't see why not, after all we both agree she doesn't have enough to do. How long do you intend to do this?" he replied.

"Well, as long as it takes to get the men back to working at the docks but I might need to have a list of names of those injured to support them. I can get the vegetables from the market," Hannah told him.

"Leave all that to me. Here's what we'll do. I'll send a trap and one of the girls to help you out. She can bring a pan of soup each day and help serve it before she comes home. Will that help?"

"Yes, perfect. Perhaps we could do soup Monday to Friday and I'll just do sandwiches and tea Saturday, and Sunday they are left to their own devices. Does that sound alright to you?"

Hannah continued her soup kitchen for a long time even when the dock was up and running again to help the families of those killed who needed help more than ever, especially as most of them came from the poorer part of town, poorer now with no money coming in.

To Hannah's joy and surprise, she married for the third time just before the harbour opened. Joy and surprise because she never thought she would marry again, her life was so busy. Joy and surprise because when asked she accepted immediately and a few weeks later she became Mrs Gabriel Brown. Not only that but she moved into the Mayor's house, the big house with just a bag of clothes. The wedding was a quiet affair with no pomp and ceremony and only close family and friends present. The reception was lunch at the house. Hannah didn't want people to think she had forgotten where she came from. As the Mayor's wife she could demand certain attention but always made time to talk to people. It was never too much trouble for her to listen to their problems, discussing what could be done with Gabriel in the evening.

Hannah had talked several times at the Literary Institute about the need to help the impoverished and to raise funds to build a hospital. The council provided her with land to build it and using the men who had previously worked on the docks, she eventually managed to build a three ward hospital with a doctor's surgery on site, named the Hannah Brown Hospital. Working with Victoria, they employed girls with limited opportunities to train as ward nurses. Life was so busy for the whole family and time seemed to pass by. Hannah had watched her girls grow into wonderful confident adults. She was very proud of all of them.

It was the fourth of May 1897 before the harbour was officially opened, much bigger and deeper than the original drawings. The land had been reclaimed so quays and warehouses could be built around the harbour itself. Everywhere in Cheapside had expanded though it was still a poor relation compared to Perth.

Hannah and her family were invited to the opening that they were all looking forward to with a carnival that was free for all those who had worked on it and their families. There was food and drink paid for by the chief engineer, the Governor and his wife.

Hannah's family were now grown up and making their own way in life. Amy-Rose was married to Robert Nelson, the manager of the large hotel that had been built close to the railway station. The young man had been smitten from their first meeting when he called into the post office to send letters for his guests. Amy-Rose teased how he came in several times, milling about before losing confidence, returning a few days later and going through similar rituals before he finally asked if she would walk out with him.

Hannah liked him immediately. He had a kind nature, keen to let her know he was a man with prospects. He endeared himself even more when he pointed his guests in the direction of the tea shop. When they married, the reception was in the hotel dining room, an intimate ceremony with no more than twenty guests.

The couple moved into an apartment at the hotel. This suited Amy-Rose as she didn't need to cook, do laundry and a minimum of cleaning. She would be the lady she always felt she should be. Her only concession was that she would remain as postmistress until a new one was in place.

Kitty had completed her training as a teacher, marrying her colleague Harry Wallace and they moved into the rooms above the shop. Their marriage was a happy affair with the schoolchildren invited to the ceremony. They opened the tea shop two evenings a week to teach adults in both English and maths. Kitty spoke out on rights for women, determined that girls would receive the same opportunities as boys. She kept in touch with Louisa Lawson, often travelling to rallies to speak on equal rights for women. Hannah was proud of all her children but Kitty had gone about her dreams in such a determined way, it gave her a warm feeling thinking about her.

Victoria studied hard to become a nurse while working in the tea shop part time. She had taken it upon herself to speak to the doctor while she was still at school, and he provided her with medical books to study. Most evenings she imparted some gruesome details to anyone who would listen. It wasn't long before she was helping the doctor on his rounds or running a clinic if he was on an emergency. When his son returned from training in England, he joined the practice and stole Victoria's heart. When she married Doctor Charlie Makin, she decamped to her in-laws where they could be on call, having a free clinic once a week.

Hannah was still owner of the post office and tea shop, the latter staffed by widows who had lost their husbands in the dock accident. Ruby was in her element running the post office, where she had an easy manner with the customers. The second hand shop was now a thing of the past but when she saw a stall on the market selling the kind of items she would have just a few years ago, she couldn't resist purchasing a little something as a reminder of how far she had come.

A letter arrived from Dan that was much more than a note

telling her she was now a grandmother to Miriam. His home was very much in America though he still sailed to England, and most important for her, his mother, was that he seemed happy. All in all she hadn't made too bad a job bringing up her family.

It wasn't all happiness for Hannah during the last few years. Within the space of twelve months first Dennis, then Maggie and finally Daniel died which was a great period of sadness. Dennis had all his children at his funeral and the church was packed with the growing Irish families. They paid for his wake and it went on long into the night. The men talked about his early life as a dissident against the Crown and how he ended up Australia. Hannah had heard some of the story before but was still surprised that this kind family man could have been such a troubled boy. Mary was very much part of the Irish family who encompassed her with open arms. Maggie's was a much quieter affair and she was finally buried with her beloved husband, Jack.

Hannah worried about Mary and her children, even approaching Gabriel about taking them in, after all there were many empty rooms in the house.

"You know this is now the Governor's house," he said. "If I lose the next election, we'll be out on the street."

"Is that likely?" Hannah asked.

"Anything's possible in politics. Have you mentioned this to Mary?

"No, I haven't but I may need to help her financially."

"You're an angel." Gabriel pulled her to him.

"Without Mary, I would have been destitute in the early years. She is the closest to family I have ever had, so I would call her an angel."

In the end Hannah did speak to Mary but she didn't want to move. Maggie had signed her house over to her so she had an income from that and Ruby's wage. She also had a stake in the timber yard which Dennis had purchased years ago so was comfortable.

Daniel also had a much quieter funeral and Hannah offered her condolences to his wife but left the organising to her. She wasn't sure how she should feel about Daniel's demise, sadness yes, but in some ways a lost opportunity for both of them. She had loved him as he had loved her once upon a time and he would always have a special place in her heart, after all he had saved her life when they first met as well as bringing Dan to her. She didn't cry but rejoiced in the friendship she had with him.

All in all Hannah thought everything had turned out well for her family in this up and coming country. There was still a lot to do but they were slowly getting themselves out of the depression following the tragedy at the docks. The school was bigger, full of children, and Hannah loved to hear them singing or playing in the sunshine. Perhaps after all this time she could think of Cheapside as home.

It was the end of the century and Queen Victoria was still ruling the world, Hannah thought how tired she must be because she certainly was. Her legs were swollen and she had a chest infection which had plagued her for months. She didn't know what was wrong with her. Gabriel kept telling her to rest, let the staff do what they are paid for, but she needed to be busy. She had seen the doctor and even Victoria had made up some awful tasting medicine for her to take but she didn't feel any better.

One of her great pleasures had been to sort out the books in the library. Her husband had given her free rein to send some to the library in the Literary Institute. Kitty took the children's books to help with adult literacy. Hannah even had a pile of books she was determined to read when she allowed herself time from committee meetings.

Sunday lunch was now at the Brown's where the children ran riot around the house. She sent everyone out into the garden while she remained on the veranda, stretched out on the chaise longue looking out to sea. She liked sitting here, watching a cinnabar sun stretch above the mist-laden trees in the early morning. But today it was the warm breeze on her skin, eyelids heavy so she allowed them to close while listening to the voices in the distance. It was such a peaceful place to be.

Her breathing calmed, shallow even, as she thought she saw someone walking toward her, their hands reaching out. As they came closer, they were smiling and she smiled back, rising to take their hand. It was Daniel to take her home.

There was a half page spread in the newspaper telling the reader about Hannah Brown, the woman who had made something of herself.

It is with deep regret we announce the death of one of the founder figures in Cheapside, Mrs Hannah Brown, wife of the mayor, Alderman Gabriel Brown who was also Chief Engineer involved in the building of the dock.

She came from nothing, but she worked tirelessly, helping women, particularly widows, to train for gainful employment. She was a great believer in education even organising fundraising events to build a hospital, the first in Cheapside.

As well as a husband, she leaves behind three daughters, Amy-Rose, Kitty and Victoria.